AF374929

Other books by Annie Russell:

The Changeling : A New Orleans Faerie Tale
(The Faerie Tale Chronicles – Book One)

The Journey Stone : A Charlevoix Faerie Tale
(The Faerie Tale Chronicles – Book Two)

The Mirror Dance: A French Quarter Faerie
Tale
(The Faerie Tale Chronicles – Book Three)

Of Ghosties and Ghoulies:
A Handbook Of Things That Go Bump In The
Night.

Drum Magic~ A Short Story

Contributing Author to:

Brigid's Flame

Acknowledgments

The following people have been instrumental in helping this book come to fruition:

Many thanks to my editor, **Emory Elgar**, for her eagle eye, love of language, and all-round good humor.
I can't thank her enough for coming along on this journey with me through the land of Faerie Tales.

Jack Russell, Jr. for his invaluable skill at formatting text and his artistic and intuitive design creations for the cover art of the books.

Many thanks to **Mary A.** who graciously allowed me, once again, the literary use and visual images of her beautiful Charlevoix home.

I am also grateful to those who taught me the strength of group magic and my even stronger fortitude in forging my own path apart from them.

~Bendith Y Mamau~

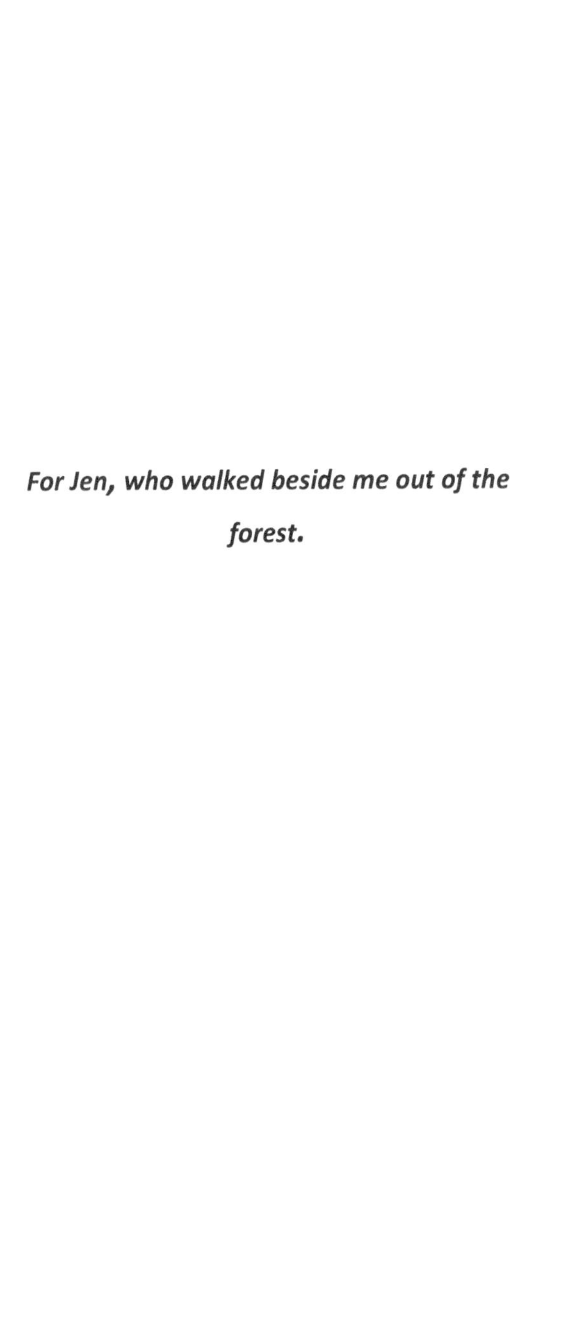

For Jen, who walked beside me out of the forest.

The Circle Call

A Witch's Faerie Tale

First hardcover edition November 2023

Edited by Emory Elgar
Layout by Jack Russell Jr.

ISBN 979-8-218-16264-1 (Hardcover)
ISBN 979-8-218-16267-2 (Paperback)

NoMi Press

annierussell.net

Chapter 1

Meredith stood in the deepening shadows as the sun descended behind the white house. The Dutch Colonial was set back from the sidewalk, sheltered by massive maples and dogwoods that were artfully planted to appear as if they had always been there—natural and effortless. In reality, her mother had designed the front yard with an eagle eye. Even the English ivy twirling about the trunk of one of the maple trees was carefully curated, encouraged to drape up and over the rough bark.

The young woman inhaled the ever-present scent of Lake Michigan's darkly undulating waters and the pungent odor of recently turned garden soil from the surrounding neighbors. The gardeners had not yet arrived, evidenced by the still-dormant run of bedding gardens that would soon overflow with pink and white impatiens. She couldn't detect the heavy perfume of the roses—the house's namesake. It was still too early and cold for the blooms to come out of hiding. Even so, Meredith knew if she stepped through the wooden gate to the right of the expansive front porch and followed the moss-covered flagstones to the back garden, she would see the banks of fully greened Rosa Rugosa plants and the buds of the beloved flowers, wrapped tight until the chilly winds off the lake warmed with the bright summer sun. For now, in early May, the sun was still a pale and anemic orb, and the breezes off Lake Michigan held the sharpness of the ice that still floated on its waters.

The porch lights flickered to life. Her feet felt like two blocks of cement anchored to the sidewalk. She knew she should take the steps into Rosehaven and out of the cold, but she couldn't seem to make her feet move. Hadn't she just made these same feet carry her over a thousand miles to the warmth of Florida and the welcoming comfort of the tiny school in Winter Park? Rollins College was as far away from where she had grown up as she could manage. Although it had taken no small number of arguments with her parents to make the trip, it was all for naught. Here she was—back at the imposing house she thought she could escape.

Upon getting the call from the Cadwell family's attorney demanding that she return to Charlevoix on the next available flight, Meredith entertained renting a small house in town or even staying in Traverse City rather than returning to the place she had so recently left. However, packing her bags and calling her professors to report that she would be gone indefinitely dropped the inescapable weight of this new reality onto her shoulders.

She knew it was pure fantasy; if she returned to Charlevoix, she would return to Rosehaven. They were a package deal. Only now her parents were no longer a part of that deal, and Meredith had yet to organize her feelings about their sudden exit from her life.

"I suppose there's no way around this," she muttered as she hoisted her heavy bags and stumbled up the uneven cobbles of the half-circle driveway.

"Dammit!" she hissed as she stubbed her toe on one of the jutting stones.

She continued to curse her shortsightedness by not having the driver pull into the turnaround and unload her bags. Her thoughts were muddled from lack of sleep and the unavoidable meeting with the attorney. When the surly ride-share driver pulled up to the curb and popped the trunk, she stepped out and grabbed her bags without giving it much thought. An additional three minutes of standing on the sidewalk staring gloomily at the house still hadn't cleared her brain fog. Only the stinging glance of her big toe against the stone brought her thoughts into focus.

"Well, here we go."

She feigned courage and skirted the imposing front porch, its columns, and huge double front doors to the smaller door just to the left. Her mother insisted on referring to it as the *service entrance*, knowing full well that many of their friends and most of the family used it as their main point of entry and exit.

Fitting the burnished brass key into the lock, the tumblers turned and clunked loudly. Meredith felt the house become aware.

"Yes, I'm home," she whispered as she stepped into the darkened vestibule.

To the right, a set of stairs lead to the lowest level of the house. Slightly to her left, a short set of steps pointed to the main floor, where the soft glow of delicate table lamps helped diffuse the darkness that permeated the rest of the house.

Meredith stepped up to the main level and dropped her key into the catch-all bowl which had sat for her entire life on a Victorian bamboo hall tree. She left her bags beside it to retrieve later. The crystal chandelier that hung suspended over the massive dining room table flickered rapidly off and on at her approach.

The light show continued as she moved into the kitchen, the overhead lights and ceiling fans swirling and dancing as she stood looking around the cavernous space.

"It's nice to see you again, too, Eliza," Meredith said with the first genuine smile she had mustered since the lawyer first called her four days prior. She didn't bother to whisper. There was no other living person within the enormous home.

"Just me, the house, and the ghosts."

The ghosts didn't make her nervous, but the unrelenting heaviness of Rosehaven settling down around her did.

"Will we ever be on good terms, you and I?" Meredith whispered to the house that was so suddenly without its Mistress.

The lights and ceiling fans had ceased their welcoming dance, and Meredith couldn't help but feel mournful. She crossed the kitchen to the bank of cupboards on the far side of the butcher's block table and extracted a pink drinking glass from the shelf that held approximately thirty-seven more.

"What in the world am I going to do with all of this stuff?"

Anxiety, held at bay for the last couple of days, rose like bile, and footfalls echoed from the floors overhead.

Gulping down her water and setting the delicately embossed glass in the drainer, Meredith stepped into the dining room and stood still. The steps sounded overhead. They paced back and forth and up and down the stairs, only to begin again in a never-ending loop of the upper floors born of the spirit's fear and its awareness of Meredith's moods.

"Eliza, it's OK. I'll take care of everything. You're still safe. I promise." Slowly, the footfalls became less erratic and eventually stopped altogether.

Meredith felt the full weight of the events that had brought her back to Rosehaven. Her head drooped as she shuffled through the butler's pantry between the kitchen and dining room, past the bamboo hall tree where she had deposited her keys, and stepped into the back stairwell. The main staircase was better-lit and quite grand, but like the smaller service door, this set of stairs was more comfortable and what she used most often. As she pulled her bags up behind her, bumping up each step, she made the landing and noticed that the small lamp perched on the delicate side table was lit. It cast reflections and refractions against the mirror inset in the large armoire that stood to its left.

"Thank you, Eliza."

She stepped into her suite of rooms, unchanged since she was a young girl. Crossing the bedroom, she opened the French doors and welcomed the whisper of the lake and its cool breezes into the stale space.

As the lace curtains danced on the chilly drafts, she pulled the duvet back and tossed the myriad of decorative pillows against the dainty Victorian settee.

Meredith, the sole remaining member of the Cadwell family, stripped down to her t-shirt and panties and climbed into the bed that, until now, she thought would only be hers as a guest at the house. Tomorrow she would meet with the attorney and find out what would happen to her—now that her parents were dead.

ROSEHAVEN

Chapter 2

Meredith sat in the attorney's austere office, listening to the explanation of her parents' deaths.

"So, as you can see, it was unavoidable. The pilot tried his hardest to make a safe emergency landing, but the plane went down too fast despite his best efforts."

Meredith nodded as the attorney, Mr. Beech, told her for the umpteenth time how she had become the only surviving member of the Cadwell family. The pilot, tasked with taking her parents to and from the small islands located off the western shore of Northern Michigan, had misjudged the amount of fuel his plane was carrying. Partway to Beaver Island, a routine and normally boring trip, the plane sputtered. While attempting to make an emergency water landing, the pilot misjudged the situation and nose-dived his plane, and its occupants, into the lake. They slammed into the frigid waters at a fatally high velocity.

"No survivors," Meredith parroted back at the elderly man sitting at the impossibly large desk across from her.

"No survivors," he repeated.

"What should I do now?"

"Go home, young lady. Your parents wrote down their final wishes in their wills decades ago. There will be some papers for you to sign eventually. For now, go home. The funeral director will stop by in a few days and talk to you about your folks' preferred arrangements. As I have said, they had settled everything years ago. I know all of this is a terrible shock, Meredith, and I'm so sorry for your loss, but try to take a little comfort in the knowledge that you'll not have to change anything should you choose. Your parents left the entire estate to you."

Meredith blinked rapidly, trying to focus on something, anything. The impossible blue of Round Lake shone in the sun outside the large window behind the lawyer. Meredith's eyes lit in desperation on the sparkling waters of the city's yacht basin.

Then, once again, she found herself standing mute and immobile in front of Rosehaven. The shadows gathered from beneath the trees as the mid-afternoon sun grew heavy and ripened into a late-afternoon orb. She had a vague recollection of leaving the offices of Beech, Beech, and McDonough, walking north by rote on Bridge Street, across the drawbridge that the main street was named for, and down the tree-lined avenue to Rosehaven. This memory, however, was foggy and indistinct. The echo of a memory of a dream.

Snatches and pieces of the meeting that she had just attended flitted through her head, ribbons floating on a breeze of disbelief and grief.

...entire estate is left to you... you don't have to do a thing...travel if you'd like... funeral arrangements are already taken care of... papers to sign later... return to Florida in the fall... Rosehaven is yours...

Meredith had very little idea of what her parents' estate encompassed aside from Rosehaven. They had purchased the neglected Dutch Colonial before she was born and spent half a decade after that restoring and transforming it into her mother's dream home. Once the structure was completed and the architect left, the designers swept in, swathing the interior with chintz, custom-made wool rugs from England, and priceless crystal-draped chandeliers. They arranged for the walls to be hand-painted rather than wallpapered. Sofas and settees were either crafted and upholstered specifically for a room or purchased at various auctions across Europe. Trips to New York resulted in the acquisitions of delicate figurines housed in the many curio cabinets and sets of fine dishes displayed in dark wooden armoires transformed into China cabinets that stood like sentinels within the formal dining room.

The bedrooms, nine in total, were outfitted with Scottish wardrobes, weighty duvets, and decorative pillows of specially curated fabrics. Goose-down throws were gathered to ward the brisk lake breezes that blew in from each room's French doors when opened to private balconies.

While there were thousands of square feet of rooms, the kitchen had always been Meredith's favorite. Still massive in scale, it felt warmed with scrubbed pine tabletops, dark green marble counters, and white-washed cabinetry. The star of the kitchen had always been the long butcher's block table that sat up to twelve people. Attached to this magazine-ready space, the sunroom had floor-to-ceiling windows, a full-sized Ficus tree in a pot that couldn't be moved without a hand dolly and three strong people, and overstuffed sofas of perfectly lived-in pink and white ticking.

The decorating was finished by the time Meredith was born. Throughout her life, nothing had changed except for her suite of rooms which evolved from a baby's nursery to a young girl's space, as well as the addition of semi-candid family photos from diving or ski trips captured in tiny silver frames that dotted every side and an occasional tabletop on the main floor. This house, the living embodiment and spiritual nexus that is—was—her mother, now belonged to her. She hoped the house was going to adjust to its new Mistress with grace, but she had her doubts. It could be quite the diva. This was not to be confused with its ghosts, most of whom Meredith was the only one privy to their existence. Eliza, in particular, had been the most active for all of Meredith's life. Though all the family members, and not a small number of guests, had experienced her presence with the lights and fans flickering off and on, footfalls walking and pacing throughout the upper floors, and the occasional movement of items from one place to another, her activities had been chalked up to squirrels that had gotten in or electrical surges. Meredith had never bothered to correct them. She felt that Eliza was best served as a family member, albeit a hidden one, and not a sideshow.

The house, though. Rosehaven was her mother's and over the years had become a bejeweled battery that gathered and amplified the thoughts, whims, and emotions of Amanda Cadwell until it was an outward expression of her interior world. Other people in residence were tolerated by the house so long as Amanda tolerated them. If the Mistress of Rosehaven found them to be tiresome, the house reacted accordingly. It made the most sensitive so uncomfortable with the oppressive and unwelcome feeling that they found a quick excuse to leave early. Alternatively, the house erupted toilets, burst light bulbs, or locked interior doors for those more obtuse. Eventually, though, all those who tried Amanda's patience were evicted by her house.

By the time Meredith traversed the choppy and turbulent waters of adolescence, she was at the top of the list of tiresome people. At the age of thirteen, she was sent to the region's most prestigious boarding school located an hour and a half away from home. For both Meredith and her mother, the distance was measured more in peace of mind than miles, and they both found the space between them a comfortable arrangement. Her father,

Jeremy, visited as often as his job allowed over her years as a student. He seemed oblivious to the cold war that continued between his wife and only child.

Meredith never didn't *love* her parents but found that being close to them, emotionally and physically, was tricky at best. Scheduled adventure vacations like skiing in Colorado or diving in the Gulf were usually picture-perfect and short. There was no need or desire to connect on any deeper level than what it took to enjoy the day's activity or the evening's dinner and show. Everyday interactions, without the distractions of exotic locations, became a field of land mines doubling as dishes left in drainers, socks on floors, or windows left open to the rain. Normal family events were fraught with hidden personal symbols known only to Amanda Cadwell, and Meredith found herself buckling under the strain of it all. Boarding school was welcomed by all. Given the atmosphere, grief for the loss of the only two people who made up her family was multifaceted, sharp, and complicated. Meredith made the conscious decision to simply not deal with any of it, for now.

Pushing open the service entry door, Meredith Cadwell announced her presence to the house with a show of bravado that she barely felt and did her best to steel herself against the heaviness she expected Rosehaven to drape around her shoulders like a mantle. Instead, there was nothing. No heaviness, no shattering of overhead light bulbs in chandeliers, and no smell of toilets that overflowed.

"Hello, house. I'm home," announced the new Mistress of Rosehaven as she strode through the dining room and into the butler's pantry where she poured herself two fingers of her father's best scotch and prepared to absolutely not deal with anything for the next day or two.

Chapter 3

The following days passed in a blur. While Meredith did manage to not think about her parents' death too deeply for a bit, the chiming of the doorbell midweek put her faux peace to an end. The arrival of the funeral director brought the unavoidable intrusion of the real world into Meredith's alcohol-fueled escape.

The attorney wasn't exaggerating when he told Meredith that her parents' funeral had already been arranged. There was nothing for her to do. Not surprisingly, Amanda Cadwell had orchestrated their funeral events down to the last detail. The flowers, music, eulogy, designs, epitaphs, and their locations within Brookside Cemetery at the family plot were all laid down in precise and unalterable language within the wills. The only thing that actually surprised Meredith was that there had been a Cadwell family plot, a detail that she was unaware of until its existence was made evident within the documents detailing her family's estate.

The funeral director assured Meredith that he had adjusted the language of the obituaries. Mr. and Mrs. Cadwell had perished together, after all, a tragic detail unforeseen by even the always-prepared Amanda Cadwell. He ensured that all the local papers would print the flowery-worded articles. He had also taken it upon himself, he said with a self-satisfied smile, to contact the designated speakers for the funeral services. As Meredith was not one of those people, her only job was to show up and look appropriately saddened at the loss of her family.

"I've taken the liberty of selecting a couple

of dates that are workable for our schedules, as well as the schedules of those speaking on behalf of your parents. I just need your final decision so the obituaries can be submitted, and the florists made aware of when and where to send the bouquets," said the small man dressed in a dark suit who perched on the sofa across from her in the main living room.

Meredith tried to remember his name, but she was uncertain about which family owned the funeral home since it had been recently sold.

At his request, she pointed at random to one of the dates circled on the printed calendar placed in front of her; she had no other commitments or obligations, so the date made no difference to her.

"Thank you, my dear. I will conclude the arrangements and be sure that all parties are made aware of the date. You don't have to worry about anything. Simply arrive half an hour early so we may seat you ahead of the guests' arrival. As you know, your parents wanted no viewing or visitation, so the service will be fairly straightforward. Their cremated remains will be interred at Brookside privately. You may attend if you wish."

Meredith noticed that, once again, she was reassured that she had nothing to worry about—that every detail was already accounted for. She was not sure whether to be grateful to her mother for her complete and utter maintenance of the estate or hurt and annoyed that she had been relegated to a bit player in the Cadwell's final social event.

Her heavy sigh, mistaken as grief by the funeral director, signaled the end of the meeting. He stood facing the young woman, who resembled her late mother to a remarkable degree.

Standing to mirror the funeral director, Meredith escorted him through the living room and into the main foyer. She smiled and thanked the gentleman for his visit and attention to detail.

She leaned against the frame of the massive double front doors and watched as he walked down the steps and opened the door to his surprisingly ostentatious red Mustang. She wasn't sure why the car felt unseemly, but she would have been more comfortable with the funeral director driving a conservatively dark sedan to match his suit.

"I suppose he can drive whatever he chooses." She admonished herself as she lifted one hand in farewell and closed the large doors against the chilly breezes of the spring afternoon.

With the return to reality, Meredith realized that she was not only hungover and headachy but strangely hungry as well. Smiling at how completely annoyed her mother would be with her slovenly ways these past couple of days, Meredith made her way to the kitchen. Some toast and a cup of hot tea with lemon were the first things on her list. Once she had something in her stomach other than scotch, she planned to take some aspirin for her head and then a warm bath for her aching body. Reality could, occasionally, have its perks.

The toast, spread with tart raspberry jam, settled into her raw stomach like a balm, and Meredith felt a bit more anchored to the present. She was almost embarrassed by her hangover and lack of participation during the meeting with the funeral director. Almost, but not quite.

"I suppose it's what happens when someone is told over and over that they have nothing to do with the current events of their own life and only need to show up for civility's sake," she muttered to the empty room.

Feeling sorry for herself wouldn't help or change the circumstances, so she finished her tea and loaded her dishes into the dishwasher. Despite it being only a few hours past noon, Meredith poured herself some water, switched off the kitchen lights, and headed for the stairs.

"Eliza, you don't care if I take an early bath and go to bed, do you?" she called to the empty house—only somewhat in jest. She smiled with relief when the lamp outside her door switched on, welcoming her into her suite.

Meredith stripped out of her days-old clothes, took one too many aspirin than recommended, and slid into the warm water in her deep bathtub. The sigh of relief turned to unexpected sobs as her physical and mental self finally released the tension and feelings that were held so taut. She stretched out as far as she could and felt the sharp emotions run through her body, wracking her frame in convulsive waves until there was nothing left but a hollowness that left her exhausted and oddly free.

As she watched the steam float around the bathroom, she heard footfalls overhead as the spirit, Eliza, reacted to the leftover tendrils of distress, pacing around and about—traversing the upper levels in a desperate bid to outrun the emotional vibrations that Meredith sent out.

As the ghost's pacing slowed, Meredith dozed in the warmth of the bathroom as images flowed behind her closed eyelids. She saw Eliza as a young wife, clad in a pretty blue gown and naively happy with her new husband. Many windows filled the large house with light. Then came visions of a heavily pregnant Eliza cowering as the shadow of her husband bore down on her. The world seemed topsy-turvy as Eliza, and Meredith as an observer, fell headlong down the main staircase, landing in a bloody heap at the bottom as a searing pain ripped through her stomach. There was nothing but blackness. Eliza floated in a dark pool of pain, knowing that her unborn child was gone.

"Oh, no! Oh, Eliza! I had no idea!" cried Meredith as she sat up from the cooling bathwater with such a start that she sent waves cascading over the edges of the tub and onto the floor. She grabbed her towel and stepped out, being careful not to fall on the now wet floor, and dried herself off.

"Is that why you're still here?" she asked as she left the bathroom for the closet just a few steps down the hall. She found her warmest pajamas and slipped them on before turning left at the intersection of the hallway of her suite to enter her bedroom. The spirit did not respond.

Meredith settled into bed, leaving the French doors open despite the chill, comforted by the weight of the down blankets. Drifting off to sleep while the sun still hung well above the horizon, she succumbed to exhaustion born of her overindulgence of alcohol and the recent emotional release. Her last thought before falling completely into oblivion was that she still didn't know if Eliza had perished at the foot of the staircase along with her unborn child.

Chapter 4

Meredith watched the spring sunshine dot the floor of the front porch as it played hide-and-seek with the Wisteria vines that provided a screen between the house and the street. The car she had called for earlier should arrive shortly. She could have walked the few short blocks to the funeral home where her parents' service was held, but she preferred the relative privacy of stepping into and directly out of the car. Privacy was also the reason she stood partly hidden by the screen of vines rather than out on the driveway. The news of her parents' death had hit the small town like a tidal wave, and Meredith felt incredibly exposed and vulnerable with the stories and talk that flowed freely within the local churches, bars, and social clubs.

With the sharp beep of the horn, her car arrived. Meredith swallowed the last of her coffee and set the mug on the table between the two white wicker settees. She smoothed her dress, put her purse over her shoulder, and walked down the steps to the waiting SUV. She felt pleased that the Cadillac Escalade was a deep, inky black with windows so tinted it was impossible to see inside. The driver nodded to her briefly as she slid into the backseat. The door closed with a heavy thunk.

Meredith stretched her legs out and crossed one ankle over the other, noting that her black pumps were already dusty.

"Good thing I didn't walk," she muttered as she peered into her compact and applied a classic red lipstick.

"Ma'am?" inquired the driver as he pulled onto Michigan Avenue.

"Sorry, just talking to myself."

There was no reply from the front seat. Meredith tipped her head back and closed her eyes during the brief ride to the funeral home. She dreaded this service on so many levels that exhaustion threatened to overtake her before it even began.

The Cadillac pulled into the parking lot and came to a smooth stop. Meredith bent down to brush the dust from her shoes and was just putting on a pair of black sunglasses designed to partially obscure her face when the driver opened the door for her. Swinging her legs out in one smooth motion, she exited the vehicle and rushed into the side entrance of the gabled building, which had served the city's dead for over one hundred years.

The hush was heavy. If an environment could be a fabric, this one would be velvet. Meredith found it off-putting. No matter the attempt at quieting them, spirits and memories of the town's past loved ones wafted through the building, sometimes slipping past like gossamer, and sometimes bumping firmly against one another before bouncing off in another direction. Had she a mind to do so, Meredith would have separated the whispers of memories from the more substantial ghosts of the place, but she couldn't do that today. She needed all her strength to keep herself to herself during the next few hours. Conversing with wandering spirits just wouldn't do, and if any of those spirits happened to be named Amanda or Jeremy Cadwell, Meredith didn't think she would be able to maintain the tenuous hold on her emotions. Losing her shit in front of half the town wasn't on her list of fun things to do in Charlevoix, the Beautiful. She was taking no chances. From her black dress to her face-shielding sunglasses, the armor was set in place to protect her from the glances and unwanted approaches of her neighbors and her parents' friends. Other protections not seen, and barely understood by Meredith, were employed as well. Stay as closed off and cold as possible. Keep emotionally separated from people and they would respond in kind. It was a technique that she had had plenty of experience with over the years.

"Hello, my dear, and welcome. The guest book is ready, and the flowers have all been delivered and arranged per your mother's instructions. Would you like to take a moment to look them over before you take your seat?"

Meredith tried not to visibly bristle at the funeral director's quietly earnest voice. While she was sure it was entirely appropriate for this time and place, it was also so obviously a fabricated cadence that was nothing if not distracting.

"No, thank you. I'm sure everything is as my mother had directed. I'll just go to my seat, please."

Taking the proffered arm, Meredith, who towered over the man by a good five inches in her heels, sauntered down the aisle created by two sections of chairs arranged in rows of six across and seven deep.

"How many people are you expecting to attend?" she asked her escort as she did the fast math in her head.

"Not to worry, Ms. Cadwell, we have additional standing room spaces for those who can't find a seat located in the back."

Meredith's stomach did an almost painful flip-flop as she added the number of chairs available and the possibility of that same amount of space for those who would be relegated to the back. Almost one hundred and fifty people! She sank gratefully into her chair at the front of the chapel, trying hard to regulate her breathing. Hyperventilating would be a mortifying public display, and she would not indulge in it, no matter what.

Still wearing the enormous black sunglasses, she looked around the space. The flowers were a riot of pink and white roses, paying homage to her mother's beloved house and gardens. Other arrangements ran the gamut from delicate carnations to gigantic green ferns. There were no coffins on the dais, but a spindly Victorian table held two ornate urns, each with a picture of its occupants propped in front of it. The effect was both simple and elegant. Meredith thought her mother would be pleased.

Hushed whispers and shuffling movements from behind let her know that the guests were arriving. She firmly resisted the urge to turn around and look, determined to maintain her attitude of aloof detachment. As there were no chairs directly beside her, it wasn't too difficult. Meredith was suddenly awash in gratitude as she understood that this seating arrangement, too, was her mother's doing.

The piped-in music sounded the processional, Lacrimosa by the Vienna Mozart

Orchestra. It was both stirring and sad, dramatic and traditional.

"Well done, mother. Well done," Meredith whispered to the picture on the dais in front of her. The photograph was easily twenty years old, but still an appropriate choice. Amanda Cadwell, smiling and tan, looked the perfect image of health and vitality. It was just the right look to counteract the idea that the very same woman was currently only so much ash and bone within the carved white urn that the picture was propped against.

"Ashes to ashes," sighed Meredith as the music dropped a notch.

The funeral director approached the front of the room to address the guests on behalf of the Cadwell family. Born away into a hypnotic state by his perfectly modulated voice, Meredith floated on waves of sadness and exhaustion buoyed by the heady scents of roses that hung in the still air of the chapel.

As her eyelids drooped behind the lenses of her sunglasses, other voices were an added counterpoint to her twilight state.

"She'll be fine," the woman said.

"But how do you know?" asked the man in a pained whisper. "It was never supposed to be like this."

"There are so many watching out for her. They are all around her. You just need to look."

"I can see them now," came the man's reply, a deep baritone full of wonder. "Have they always been there?"

"Yes", always."

"Does she know?" Jeremy Cadwell asked his wife.

"Sometimes," replied Amanda with a warmth in her voice her family rarely heard when she was alive.

Meredith stirred as the speaker changed from the carefully neutral tone of the funeral director to the neighbor who lived across the street from Rosehaven.

Despite her best attempt, Meredith jumped with her sudden awareness of the present moment and cried softly, "Mother?"

The elderly woman stopped her squeaky monologue to smile sadly at Meredith, then resumed her recollections of what glorious neighbors her parents had been.

Meredith's thoughts raced. Had she really heard her parents? If so, were they talking about her? Was it just wishful thinking caused by grief and exhaustion?

The service seemed to drag on as speaker after speaker approached the front of the room to offer eulogies and thoughts about the Cadwells and their tragic deaths. Meredith thought she might scream in frustration; most of these people had never been close family friends but rather people vying for invitations to the exclusive fundraising events that were often held at Rosehaven.

Most, but not all. After an unknown real estate agent pontificated about various fishing and golf outings with her father, Meredith was gladdened to see Rachael Thompson's approach. Rachael and Amanda were as close as two friends could be, having grown up and attended grade school and university together. Rachael was quiet and even-keeled compared to Amanda's headstrong ways, endearing each to the other. One lock to one key.

After what seemed an eternity, the recessional song sounded, On Eagle's Wings. As the guests filed solemnly out of the chapel, Meredith thought that this might have been the only wrong-footed decision on her mother's part. While even Amanda Cadwell couldn't have predicted her death at the failure of an airplane designed to hold her aloft, she thought it gruesomely ironic that the funeral director still kept this hymn in the service.

As the last of the attendees moved out into the lobby to chat and sign the guest book, Meredith slipped quietly out of the side door from which she had entered and into the cavernous Cadillac that would deposit her back home. She knew perfectly well that she was expected to be the one and only participant in the traditional receiving line, but she simply couldn't fathom the fortitude it would take to do so.

Chapter 5

Meredith found a suitable location on the back porch for the last of the massive ferns. The plants had been delivered to Rosehaven after the funeral. She shaded her eyes from the glare of the late-May sunshine and reveled in the unlikely warmth of the day. Eighty-degree weather before June wasn't the norm, but it was welcomed by most of the full-time residents who were more than ready to say goodbye to the winter's cold and gray.

The ferns added a note of summer to the back porch. Meredith was grateful for them. Arranging the seasonal foliage used to be her mother's domain. She knew the information for the previous years' orders must be on her desk, but she didn't feel up to tackling the project.

"If only the floral arrangements could be rooted, I'd be all set," she said as she scooted a wicker chair out of the way of the new fern.

Meredith had donated almost all the funeral arrangements to the hospital and the local retirement home. While Rosehaven was plenty large enough to take in every single one of them—plus some—she thought it rather sad they would have been housed within a basically empty home until they wilted and died. When she voiced her thoughts to Mr. Beech, he suggested donating them. She thought it was the perfect way to share the enormous number of colorful blooms and agreed. She did, however, keep a small spray of the pink and white roses arranged by her mother. She planned on drying them and keeping them in her sitting room, along with the memorial pamphlet and guest book.

Still feeling rundown and tired from the recent events that uprooted her life so completely, Meredith decided that an early dinner and an evening watching brainless TV sounded perfect. She cast one last admiring glance at the beautiful ferns and the formal knot garden, which had been Amanda Cadwell's pride and joy. It spread out from the long back porch, a mirror image of the one spanning the front of the house, the boxwood borders ever green. The smaller interior gardens that were sectioned off were still barren of the perennial flowers that would soon attract bees, butterflies, and songbirds to the back of Rosehaven. Sighing at the enormity of the work and responsibility now laid at her feet, she headed inside through the tall French doors that lead to the sunroom and the adjacent kitchen.

"Hello, house!"

Meredith felt better after sending out a greeting as she entered. She didn't feel unwelcome any longer, but she often felt the heaviness of being the only living being within its cavernous space.

"Maybe I should get a cat? Or a dog? Oh, hell, I can't even get my act together to order plants! What am I thinking?"

Picking through the refrigerator reminded her that she had not gone shopping since her arrival, so her options were limited. She pulled out some bread that had seen better days, a brick of Colby-Jack cheese, and a bunch of wilted green onions. Her parents were more inclined to eat out than cook for themselves, so the food in the house was a selection of various snacks and lunch items. Meredith had never been an enthusiastic eater, finding it tiresome, so a simple sandwich sufficed.

She sliced the cheese as thin as possible, spread mayo on each side of the bread, and placed each slice—mayo side down—in the skillet that was heating on the stove. She layered the cheese, chopped onions, and sprinkled on a dash of dried thyme and cracked black pepper—the whole of her culinary skills. However, it resulted in a tasty sandwich. Flipping until each side was golden and the cheese melted, she transferred it from the pan to a plate, added a handful of potato chips and some grapes, and headed to the main living room.

At first glance, the room appeared overly formal. It was outfitted with matching overstuffed chintz sofas, a velvety wine-hued ottoman that doubled as a coffee table, and a crystal chandelier holding court overhead. After further inspection, though, it was actually quite a comfortable room. The down sofas were soft and invited stretching out. The ottoman was large enough to accommodate plates, glasses, and magazines, and the smaller side tables held sentimental family photos in silver and burnished bronze frames. The huge armoire that dominated an entire wall, when opened, was retrofitted with a large TV and sound system, making the room a perfect space to lounge and watch television or listen to music.

Exactly how Meredith planned to spend the rest of her evening. She opened the doors to the armoire, located the remote controls, and settled onto the sofa—positioned directly in front of the screen to select the night's escape. Sandwich and chips at hand, she flipped through channels until she found a true-crime series that she hadn't seen before. Meredith happily lost herself in the simple dinner and the televised misery of strangers.

On the second floor, two ornate Art Deco bronze statues of filmy-gowned women framed the half-moon windows that dominated the first landing of the main staircase. Identical in detail and hailing from a long-gone French chateau, each held a glass globe aloft in perpetual adoration. As Meredith cuddled into the down sofa in the living room and lost herself in crimes of passion and betrayal, Eliza—well versed in betrayal and violence—began her self-appointed job of switching on the evening lights. The statues' globes flickered on with a soft glow that radiated out onto the street as the spirit glided past. Shortly after, the small lamp outside of Meredith's rooms shone a watery yellow light as did its twin, located at the other end of the second-floor landing outside of the late Mr. And Mrs. Cadwell's suite. Over the years, Eliza's light shows went unquestioned by two of the three people living in Rosehaven. Amanda believed that either Jeremy or Meredith switched the lamps on in the evening, and Jeremy thought it to be Amanda or Meredith. Meredith, however, always knew it was Eliza and always made sure to thank her.

Tonight was no exception. As Meredith turned off the television and closed the heavy doors to the armoire, the first floor was plunged into darkness except for the gentle glow of the lamps that led her safely up the main staircase and to her rooms.

"Thank you, Eliza. Sleep well."

Chapter 6

 ather Francis Greene stared at the hastily penciled note scrawled on a scrap of his notepad; he was beyond dumbfounded.

"Her name is Ashlynne, and she needs a home."

That was it. No signature, no explanation of where she came from or how she had gotten there.

Father Greene looked around his small office, half hoping to see an intruder—one who had recently carried a red-haired toddler—crouching in a corner or hiding behind the drapes, but there was no one.

He looked down at the little girl who slept deeply and unconcerned by her own mystery.

She appeared to be about two years old and was covered with his afghan, a recent gift from the Ladies Auxiliary—an atrocious thing sporting uneven stitches of a hue that used to be called 'harvest gold' offset with the incongruous color choice of deepest purple. His new house guest appeared uninjured and healthy, though poorly dressed in pinafore and woolen tights. Her shoes seemed to be several sizes too large, and the Father suspected that they had originally belonged to an older sibling. There was something old-fashioned and shabby about her clothing, though it was all fairly clean with no rips or holes.

"Someone has loved and cared for this child," whispered the priest to the empty room. "How did she come to be here?"

And at that, the little girl's eyes popped open, her mouth gaped, and a wail of fear, frustration, and hunger poured forth. Until now, Father Greene has never experienced the full force of a toddler's emotions. Priest or not, Francis Greene was an adult human, and adult humans were often hard-wired to respond to such cries.

The priest emitted a cry of his own, "Mrs. Boyle! Mrs. Boyle—come quickly!"

Ashlynne's cries wove in and out of Father Greene's yelling, a powerful cacophony not heard within the rectory in decades that summoned the requested help of Mrs. Boyle. She ran through the office door and slid to a halt, shocked at the sight. Her boss waved his arms at a small child, both of them yelling themselves blue in the face.

"Stop! Stop!" cried the confused woman, not caring which of them stopped as long as at least one of them did. Her head was beginning to pound.

Seeing his secretary skid into his office, Father Greene stopped yelling, though Ashlynne did not. His blue eyes, normally crinkled and bright with the next smile or laugh that was ready to pour forth from his open and friendly face, were now wide and scared. No smiles and definitely no laughter.

"Do something!" he begged his secretary, waving his arms at the wailing bundle of harvest gold and purple on his sofa.

Pushing past her employer, Mrs. Boyle expertly scooped up the distraught toddler, resting the red head against her shoulder, and patted her back in the universally accepted method of soothing a crying child. Adding the bounce-and-walk technique with a rhythmic 'shhhshhhshhh' whisper eventually reduced the crying to hitching hiccups.

"Now then," said Mrs. Boyle to the glassy-eyed priest sitting splay-legged on his desk chair. "Where did this child come from?"

"I have no idea."

Still bouncing, walking, and shushing, she eyed her boss. "What does that mean, Father? When I left for lunch—your order is in the kitchen, by the way—there was no child here.

Now there is. It had to have come from somewhere!"

"She."

"What?"

"She's a she, not an it," murmured Father Greene, staring at the wall.

"Fine, she. She must have come from somewhere."

"I imagine she did, but I don't know from where. I returned from washing my hands and here she was, sleeping on the sofa, covered in that hideous afghan that the Ladies Auxiliary gave me."

Mrs. Boyle shot the priest a hard glance. "My niece helped make that for you."

"Yes, well," Father Greene trailed off. He really didn't care who made it. He was more concerned with how the toddler wound up under it. On his sofa.

"Mrs. Boyle, have any of the women or older girls had a baby recently? Maybe from an inauspicious or unplanned encounter?"

"Father, this child is easily twenty-four months old. The hypothetical woman, or girl, that you're wondering about would have been pregnant and given birth over two years ago! Why give the child up now?"

"Maybe the father hasn't been in the picture and the shame became too great?"

"Exactly what year do you think this is?" snapped Mrs. Boyle, tilting her head to better level her steely stare at him. "On this island, I would make a bet that a good number of weddings have a child in attendance, just not one to be seen by you for five to six months after the nuptials. That being said, even without a wedding, we don't hide young women away in shame anymore. You should know this."

"Yes, well, I suppose so," whispered the priest, duly chastised. He made a mental note to pay closer attention to the dates of weddings and baptisms from here on out.

"And, in case you've not been paying attention for all these years, this is a small island—very small. There's not a birth or death that goes without notice around here. I've never laid eyes on this child, have you?"

"No, I haven't, which doesn't help me at all to answer your question of where she came from," came the clergyman's weary response.

Ever practical, Mrs. Boyle patted her boss on the shoulder and walk-bounced herself, and the now content toddler, to the kitchen.

"Well, wherever she came from, it had to have been a while ago. I can feel her little tummy growling. This little one is hungry!"

The priest sat staring at the sofa that had recently held the mysterious red-haired toddler wearing strangely old-fashioned clothing.

"Gran would have said she was a fairy changeling," he mused aloud.

He rarely thought of his Irish-born great-grandmother. She died when he was just entering grade school, but he sure would have liked her to be here right about now. There was something otherworldly about the girl's arrival. He doubted anyone in these modern times would know enough of the Old Ways to offer an explanation.

"We'll call her Ashlynne Barrow," he called into the kitchen.

"She's not a stray cat that you can just adopt and name, you know," replied his secretary, who had reappeared in the kitchen doorway.

Ashlynne was quiet now and happily sucking on a slice of apple.

"I'm well aware, but she will need a last name."

"May I ask why you chose that one?"

"A barrow is a fairy hill, a place where the Good Folk come into our world from their own. My Gran used to tell me about them. She said that, back in Ireland, you had to be very careful not to enter one unaware or you would wander into their world only to reenter your own—hundreds of years from when you began."

"And you think this child came here from a fairy hill in Ireland?"

Father Frances could hear the laughter that his secretary was trying unsuccessfully to keep from her voice, but it didn't bother him. She wouldn't understand.

"Not really, but I suspect this little girl has traveled farther than you or I will ever know. And she needs a name. Ashlynne was given to her by whoever left her in our care. Barrow seems as good as any for a last name, and my Gran would approve. So, Barrow it is."

Mrs. Boyle nodded slowly as the child in her arms happily gnawed on the wedge of apple. She had not missed the use of 'us' in her boss's statement and knew that she, already a grandmother herself, would now be a godmother—of sorts—to this orphaned toddler.

Neither Mrs. Boyle nor the priest saw the enormous owl take flight from outside the window where it was sent to observe the arrival of Ashlynne Barrow to the village of St. James on Beaver Island, located in the cold, dark waters of Lake Michigan.

Chapter 7

As the spring gave way to early summer, Meredith felt more and more focused on what she should do in the fall. The responsible thing would be to go back to Florida and Rollins College. She would need to retake a good number of classes due to leaving early in the last semester, but that didn't bother her as much as trying to feel motivated to enter the world of college courses, study groups, and coffee shops again. The responsible thing and the desirable thing weren't always the same, so Meredith spent weeks vacillating with her plans. Knowing that the deadline to enroll and sign up for classes was fast approaching only made it all the more frustrating.

There were days when she was all but set to call Student Services and re-enroll. She missed her small group of friends and the camaraderie of the misfits who gathered to study for exams and endure endless lectures. Fast on the heels of those memories, though, were images of draining coffee cup after coffee cup to stay awake just a bit longer to cram for a test, trying to join groups of her fellow students for bar hopping and breakfasts at two in the morning—only to be snubbed because her family didn't come from the type of wealth that was standard there. Her peers came from opulent lifestyles, second homes in the Turks and Caicos, skiing in Vale, and shopping trips to Paris. Meredith knew her family was well-to-do by most standards, but Rollins' students put her family's finances to shame. They never hesitated to let her know she didn't quite measure up. Her parents often said she was overly sensitive and that her classmates couldn't possibly mean to make her feel lesser, but Meredith had her doubts.

Flipping through the date book that sat open next to her, Meredith saw that her time to dilly-dally with her student status was almost up.

"Ugh. Why can't this be an easier decision? I mean, I suppose I could just flake out and not go back, but that seems so wrong," she said to the empty kitchen as she rinsed out her coffee cup and left it in the drainer.

The clank of the brass mail slot let her know that the day's mail had arrived. Walking briskly through the butler's pantry and down the steps to the service door, Meredith scooped up the drift of envelopes and magazines. After flipping through catalogs, insurance leaflets, and fliers for political candidates, Meredith dropped the pile of unwanted mail into the kitchen trash. She sat down at the table to inspect the remaining mail that she deemed necessary or interesting.

The letter from the attorney's office only detailed the charities that her parents would like her to continue; she would call them with her decision later. The next letter was from the insurance company that had held her parents' life insurance policies. The letter explained how they had settled the claim and closed the account, all detailed in crisp and impersonal legalese that seemed clear enough, but Meredith added it to the stack for the attorney. Best to speak to him about it and make certain that everything was in order. The next item was a print of a hand-drawn advertisement in simple black and white. Suns, moons, stars, and a myriad of swirls and dots made up the printed page's border, the effect being decidedly celestial. The printing within announced an open invitation to hear a speaker who promised an evening of interesting discussions, exchanges of ideas, and fellowship in a 'safe space for those of like mind.'

Meredith wasn't sure if she felt intrigued or simply bored and lonely, but she thought she might go see what this speaker had to say. Not sure if she was 'of like mind' since she didn't know the speaker's mind, she decided that if she went, she would simply listen.

The date for the event said June 21, tomorrow.

"Well, I suppose I could adjust the tons of social obligations that I have," she muttered sarcastically as she circled the date and tacked the flier to the front of the refrigerator—an action her mother had detested.

"Sorry," whispered Meredith as she headed outside to the garden, still contemplating her plan for college.

The next day dawned bright and warm, the morning sun dancing between the lace curtains that hung at the tall windows which made up the sunroom's exterior walls.

Meredith sipped her coffee as she re-read the artsy flier for the hundredth time, trying to decide if she was making the right decision to attend.

'Of like mind' is pretty vague, she thought. She noted the drawings of bees, smiling suns, and winking moons along the edges of the cheap stationery—copy paper. Hidden amongst the more obvious drawings were sketched female forms with arms held aloft, five-pointed stars, and what appeared to be various astrological symbols. The effect was of a black and white tapestry drawn in a hurry, but by someone with no small amount of artistic talent.

"I mean, serial killers and dairy farmers have groups of like-minded people..." her voice trailed off as she tried to envision what type of gathering had people interested in bees and smiling suns.

Gardeners?

Meredith rolled her eyes at herself. She would either show up and see what the group held in combined interests or stay home and continue to worry about whether she should return to school.

"OK, I'm going. If it really is a gathering of dairy farmers, I can just leave, right?"

As she headed back upstairs to shower and dress, she wondered what she would do if it was a group of serial killers, but chided herself for being silly.

"What you need, Meredith, is a sign," she said to herself. "You cannot decide what to do with yourself sitting in the house day in and day out. So, you're going to get dressed and go see what this gathering is all about. And then you're going to go to the next event that is put in your path, and you will do this for the next ten days. At the end of the ten days, you'll have made up your mind about whether to leave and go back to Florida or stay here."

The lights above her head flickered and danced as she made her way up the stairs to the second floor.

Meredith smiled.

"Sound like a plan, Eliza?"

The heavy wooden door of her suite closed as the footfalls of the spirit paced back and forth as she walked an endless loop of the third floor above Meredith's rooms.

As the antique Tiffany grandfather clock in the main foyer chimed the half hour, Meredith hurried down the service stairs, sandals slapping on the hardwood risers. Her wet hair was braided back and out of her face, and the simple ankle-skimming black skirt swished around her legs as she tucked her heather gray t-shirt into the elastic waistband. Her mother would have chastised her choice of clothing, citing the lack of color, but Meredith chose the outfit specifically to not draw attention to herself. Grabbing her purse and donning her favorite enormous black sunglasses, she left the house through the service door and unlocked her mother's—now her—car. Meredith consulted the written directions, started the car, and pulled out of the semi-circular drive. She headed north to the tiny village of Horton Bay. Despite her fear of serial killer-dairy farmers, she was excited to go somewhere new. It was the first step in her ten-day plan about how to proceed with her life.

Meredith turned left off of the main highway onto a scenic county road that wound around small golf courses and bucolic farms. Eventually, the blue waters of Lake Charlevoix peaked through the dense tree line to her right. The road signs warned her to slow her speed to twenty miles per hour. She bumped her car slowly over the tiny bridge that spanned Horton's Creek and arrived in the don't-blink-or-you'll-miss-it village. At a gentle turn off of the main street, a small yard flag with a sun and moon on its indigo background signaled her turn. There was no street sign and not much of a street. There was a packed dirt road that led off into the dense foliage of birches, field grass, and stately old-growth maple trees. After creeping slowly down the dirt road for almost three miles, the road made a wide, almost U-turn, and an unassuming brick ranch appeared sitting alone in a green lake of field corn. At least a dozen cars were parked sporadically along the road, allowing anyone needing to leave space to pull out and back down the unmarked road to the main street.

"Well, here I go," whispered Meredith, unable to shake the feeling that she was making a life-altering decision instead of simply attending a small gathering to hear a local speaker.

Stop overreacting, she thought to herself as she adjusted her sunglasses and walked up the packed dirt drive to the front door.

Chapter 8

It was almost one in the morning when Meredith pulled into her driveway and let herself into the house. She hadn't planned on staying at the gathering very long, let alone for over six hours, but she found herself swept up in the laughter and conversation until she could no longer resist the sleepiness that descended upon her like a warm sweater. Despite being encouraged to stay, the drive home seemed daunting, and she thought it best to make her exit while she was still awake enough to do so.

Once home, she felt tired but, also, as if a part of her hummed like a tuning fork, repeatedly struck. Her eyes skittered off of surfaces before she could focus. Her feet tapped and bounced, and her skin seemed to feel every atom of the air in the room. Even her hands wouldn't hold still, her fingers twining and twitching over and over again.

Meredith felt alive and engaged for the first time in years.

She paced the house from top to bottom, folded some laundry left in the dryer, unloaded the dishwasher, and watered the Ficus tree until the buzzy feeling wore off a bit, though not entirely.

"Three in the morning! Oh, my god, tomorrow—uh, today—is going to be rough if I don't get some sleep!"

The elation she felt earlier had downgraded to just feeling twitchy, like she had had too much caffeine too late in the day. Meredith decided that if anything would help to calm her down, a hot bath would.

It was almost five in the morning by the time she climbed out of the tub and into bed, finally feeling more calm and much more sleepy. As she closed her eyes, images from the previous evening flickered past like a movie with a particularly disjointed plot. She watched visions of the shabby, but still comfortable, house that belonged to Tom Mitchell, the man who had organized the event. Tom was a larger-than-life person who purposely portrayed himself to be a man's man. With his 6'4" frame and deep voice, he easily commanded the attention of an entire room. The faces of the other guests flowed past as her breathing slowed and deepened. She envisioned the older woman with the halo of brilliant white hair who had drawn the fliers and her husband who used his smile to hide a brittle and easily offended nature. Meredith also thought of another woman who made continual references to the Indigenous People of the area and their superior-to-all-else spiritual practices, though she was blonde-haired and blue-eyed. The woman's laugh, though, was genuine, and her eyes sparkled. Then there was the gigantic gentleman who looked to be a dangerous outlaw biker but proved to be a soft-spoken and gentle nurse's assistant in one of the local nursing homes. There were easily a dozen or more people in attendance at the event, but Meredith had a hard time remembering all of their faces, let alone any names. A few conversations stuck with her, though.

"Of like mind" turned out to be people who had an interest in the occult and the mysterious. Their host introduced himself as a 'traditionally trained Witch.' Rather than feeling afraid, Meredith felt a little embarrassed for him and his ludicrous claim. The others in attendance mostly smiled and nodded, so she followed their lead, still determined to not draw undue attention to herself.

When asked to elaborate, Tom held court, regaling the group with stories of his studies and training, all of which bordered firmly on the side of embellishment—if not outright fantasy. Having finished his training, he said he began to reach out to the community in order to gather together the local Witches, Wiccans, and Pagans. This led to a lengthy, spirited, and—in Meredith's opinion—confusing discussion and debate about what a Pagan and Wiccan were, versus what a Witch was, and who could claim these titles. While she had no previous knowledge of occult studies, Wicca, Paganism, or magic, Meredith found herself caught up in the energy of the group and happily joined in with what little of the discussion she was able to comprehend. Though she knew next to nothing about these topics, not one person in the group made her feel that she didn't belong. In fact, her complete lack of previous knowledge seemed to endear her to the group.

As Meredith finally slipped into a much-needed sleep, her last conscious thought was wondering why that was the case; why would a shy young woman who had zero previous knowledge of the topics up for discussion be welcomed so completely and without question?

It wasn't the bright afternoon sunshine, the sound of a jackhammer from the construction happening next door, or the birds that called incessantly outside her window that finally roused Meredith from her bed. It was thirst. Her tongue felt like wool that had been glued to the roof of her mouth, and her teeth felt like pebbles left in the hot sun for too long. Even her eyes felt dry and scratchy.

Stumbling from bed and into her bathroom, she held her hair back and gulped water directly from the tap until her stomach felt bloated and queasy.

"Oh, I knew today was going to be rough, but I feel awful," she moaned as she stuffed her legs into a pair of ancient sweatpants and shook her hair out of yesterday's braid.

Meredith yanked her duvet back into place and piled the decorative pillows back onto the head of the bed to deter herself from simply climbing back in and hoping to become comatose once again.

"This is the worst hangover ever," she whined as she stumbled down the stairs to the kitchen. Her stomach lurched as she contemplated coffee, so she put the kettle on to boil and opted for some tea instead.

Sitting in the sunroom sipping the gentle chamomile infusion, Meredith tried to get a handle on why she was feeling so terrible. She had had no alcohol and only snacked on a few crackers. Therefore, no matter how it felt, this wasn't a hangover or food poisoning. Crawling into bed at just before dawn could account for some of her illness, but certainly not to this degree.

The jangle of the phone ripped her from her thoughts and left her holding her head in pain.

"Ugh, ugh, ugh. Why?" she moaned as she stumbled to the phone, unsure whether she would answer it or tear it off the wall. Anything that stopped the horrid noise would suffice.

"Huh-lo," she muttered, opting to answer the call rather than destroy the phone.

"MEREDITH CADWELL!" the voice on the other end boomed, causing Meredith to squint her eyes closed from the pain in her head. "IT'S TOM MITCHELL!"

"Oh, my god, why are you yelling?" she replied in as icy a tone as she could manage around the thundering headache that threatened to send her to her knees.

Tom merely laughed and then continued as if she hadn't said a word, a habit that she would become more acquainted with than she currently thought possible.

"Yes, uh huh, OK..." she muttered, more to get him off the phone than anything else, and hung up at his next breath.

As she slumped into the softness of the sunroom's down-stuffed sofa and burrowed under the Afghan that she pulled off the back of the closest chair, she realized that she had just agreed to attend Tom's newly formed study group tomorrow.

She moaned softly and let herself fall back into the softness of sleep, deciding that she would make a plan about her attendance when she awoke.

Chapter 9

The room became indistinct as Meredith maintained her focus on the scrying bowl in front of her. The ornately inscribed silver vessel had an inky black interior that, when filled with water, gave the illusion of a bottomless pool.

The shabby sofa and scuffed coffee tables of Tom's living room drifted away as if swept aside by the smoke from the incense that billowed forth from the small cast-iron cauldron that sat to the left of the scrying bowl. The small sighs and occasional throat clearings of the other group members sounded far away and inconsequential as Meredith looked down and through the blackness rather than simply at its surface.

The ten-day deadline to decide whether to return to school came and went months ago. She had asked for a sign and felt that her newfound community of friends was sign enough. Why go to a place where she more often than not felt excluded, leaving behind a place where she finally felt that she belonged?

The weekly study group at Tom's, now moving into its sixth month, had become the central post around which her other days revolved. So caught up was she in this new community of people who believed in magic and spells, Gods and Goddesses, spirits, and energy. It surprised her to learn that she was one of the few members who could regularly see and communicate with spirits without the aid of tools and spells. This ability was something that had always been a part of her, and it had never occurred that she was one of only a few people who had the skill. Her family life, being uncommunicative at best, didn't provide a space for discussion of spirits, spirituality, or the occult, so Meredith wandered through her world—seeing things others didn't– not understanding that this was unique. At school, her friends chided her about her 'hunches,' but that was all. There were no discussions about what she knew, how she knew, and why they didn't.

Within the study group, there were always discussions, debates, and endless theories about abilities, the use of energy, how spells work, ancient herbalists, and whether 'the burning times' in Europe were real or exaggerated. Meredith's innate abilities were not only up for discussion but encouraged to thrive and evolve within the safety of those with a 'like mind.' Scrying, the use of a reflective surface to see visions, had become one of her more potent abilities, and the group often asked her to look for answers to their questions or theories.

Tonight, Meredith searched the depths of the scrying bowl for guidance about where the group should head in the future. Tom felt strongly that the members were ready to expand past an informal study group, but others were not sure if it was the best timing. Meredith, herself, had no real opinion on the matter but agreed to scry for any available messages or visions that would help to make the most advantageous choice for them all.

Moving her view further into the watery depths before her, she felt her body slump as her consciousness flowed over the rim of the silver bowl and slid into the still pool of water within. Diving deeper, Meredith sought the images that could provide guidance and direction for her group of friends.

Time and place had no meaning within the depths of the silver bowl. As Meredith slid further into the blackness, scraps of images slid by—visions and scenarios not currently meant for her or her quest. After watching a bouquet of daisies tied with a pink ribbon float past, she noticed the surrounding air had become lighter and weak sunlight illuminated a vast green field.

Meredith felt her toes grip the lush grass as she stepped into the vision. The sky was the early morning blue-gray of post-dawn, and the dew had not yet dried, though the breezes were warm and fragrant. A rough linen robe or gown, she wasn't sure which, touched the top of her bare feet, and a similar linen cloth covered her hair.

In front of her was a stone wall with an arched wooden door cut into it, bound with heavy strips of iron and an enormous keyhole. From inside the wall, Meredith could hear women's voices singing, a gentle wave of female adoration and devotion.

As she stood there, barefoot and robed, the voices grew louder and less gentle. The singing became a strident chanting, both forceful and aggressive, making it even more powerful in its femininity. The hairs on Meredith's arms stood on edge, and she fought the urge to leave this place. However, though it was an unnerving energy, she remained confident that this vision held the key to answering her question. So, she stood tall and still, unsure if the people in the vision could see her, or if she was only a shadow in the morning gloom.

The voices rang out as the heavy wooden door opened, and a line of women filed out. Each was mantled as she was and clothed in a robe such as hers, cinched at the waist with a rough hemp cord. Each one held aloft a lantern from which shone a bright flame. A small woman, her mahogany curls escaping her mantle, lead the group, her voice flowing out and her arm raised, holding aloft a lit lantern.

One after another, they marched forth from the walled structure and into the field where Meredith stood. None seemed to notice her, and for that, she was grateful. As the sun struggled to fully illuminate the sky, the women approached an ancient oak tree—the only tree that could be seen for miles—and surrounded it seamlessly. To Meredith, this looked to be an activity that was well-known and well-practiced.

The last woman to make her way around the circle became the first to lift her lantern to hang it upon the nearest branch, then so on and so on, each woman hanging her light on the branch closest to her until the only woman left holding a lamp was the one who had led them.

The enormous oak tree's lowest branches twinkled and sparked with the lamps hung there as the voices of the women grew, becoming a sickening shriek. Meredith wanted so badly to cover her ears. The high-pitched screams were so different from the gentle singing that had first alerted her to the group.

The leader set her lantern down on a flat rock in front of her and raised both arms over her head as the screeching of her sisters continued unabated. Meredith watched, eyes wide and frightened, as the dark-haired woman produced a large sword from her robes and held it straight over her head, the hanging lanterns sending their light to wink and dance off the blade. The woman to the left of the sword-bearer stepped forward and produced a wound-up bundle of cord, utterly plain and unassuming, yet Meredith felt cold and sick at the sight of it. The bundle was placed on the rock next to the lantern and, as one, the group's keening dropped to a deep murmur that rumbled and shook Meredith to her core. The leader of the group swung the blade down and impaled the cord, slicing through the mass and cutting it in two. The murmuring stopped.

Having set the heavy sword aside, the leader of the group bent and retrieved the lantern and the severed cords, each to a hand. At the sight of this, the group chanted, low, in a language that Meredith didn't know, but the energy was forceful and potent. The pace of the chant increased in both speed and volume until Meredith was sure she would turn and run screaming, so uncomfortable it made her. Just as it hit an almost unbearable crescendo, the mass of cords was shoved into the lantern and set afire, flaring brightly and consumed almost immediately. As the hemp mass burned into ash, Meredith felt sick—dizzy, ill, and confused. The chanting had stopped, but the ringing silence only added to her discomfort.

The first to leave the circle, the leader walked out and around the tree, each woman following her in silence, their lanterns remaining in the ancient oak tree—flickering in the brightening morning. As the line of women filed past her, Meredith saw the leader turn back and fix her with a sly smile that made her blood run cold, then winked. Holding Meredith's gaze, the dark-haired woman patted the cord around her waist, dipped her chin in acknowledgment, and turned to face the heavy wooden door through which she led her group.

As Meredith tumbled head over heels in a violent expulsion from the vision, it occurred to her that, while she was dressed just as the other women, she was missing one piece of the utilitarian costume. She wore no cords about her waist.

She came to a bone-jarring crash in complete darkness. There was no light and no sound, just a feeling of immense space that was both profound and intimate. Meredith sat extremely still, unsure about how to proceed. With no sense of time, she had no idea how long she sat in the infinite darkness. At some point, she noticed a silvery glimmer. She stood and reached out, the gossamer silver thread surprisingly sturdy in her hand. Tugging at it, she saw from the depths of the dark a blooming of yellow and white—a swirl of color that moved and gyrated as it made its way directly toward her.

"I am very tired of standing my ground," Meredith muttered as she fought the urge to move out of the way of the vortex that swooped quickly down the silver thread in her direction.

And then it landed, literally. Meredith felt the weight of the giant bird and its sharp talons as it lit on her shoulder, impossibly large and incredibly beautiful. The silver thread hung loosely around one great talon, the other end looped around Meredith's wrist.

The owl stared at its Mistress with intelligent, cold eyes and bobbed its head in greeting.

"Hello, there. You are an amazing creature," crooned Meredith as she stroked the owl's head, slowly and carefully to not startle the bird of prey that sat so close to her face.

The owl blinked, long and slow, and settled itself more firmly on its Mistress's shoulder.

"Shall we go, then?" Meredith asked the owl as she closed her eyes and felt herself drop back into her body in the living room of her friend Tom. The owl settled securely within her breast was unseen and unnoticed by anyone within the group.

Chapter 10

Dark Grove Coven was born from the misinterpretation of a vision; a group gathered together based on what they desired to be truth rather than the truth itself. Moreover, it met as a coven for the first time on a Monday, a day dedicated to the moon herself. Everyone knows that Mondays are the easiest days to get lost in mists of fantasy or to be caught in webs of paranoia and fear. Those traveling the way of the moon must be ever vigilant that they don't jump high over pebbles or walk blithely into boulders.

All is not as it seems when the moon is dominant.

"But that's not how it *felt*!" Meredith protested. She was tired of going over this time and again.

"Meredith," Tom began in a voice that said 'I am so much older than you, and a trained Witch, and therefore I know best.' "We asked you to scry for guidance about our future as a group, and your vision was of a group participating in a magical ritual. It couldn't be plainer."

"Tom, visions are not plain. They are not simple. Visions don't offer a yes or no answer. This vision had a feel to it that was not pleasant! The group was engaged in a hurtful ritual. It scared me."

Try as she might, Meredith couldn't share the sinister feeling from the vision with Tom or the group. They didn't see as she did, so they didn't understand the subtle nature of it all. What scared her the most, though, was that the scene seemed to be intimate and personal, and the leader of the group of women actually saw her and interacted with her. It had made her feel terrified in a way she couldn't explain, so she didn't. She also didn't tell the group about the owl. She wasn't sure why, but it seemed important that she keep this to herself.

Between a refusal to acknowledge an unwanted truth and the inability to provide an accurate accounting of the vision, a narrative was put forth that allowed the coven to be actualized. Under the murky energies of the moon on a Monday, a group mind developed.

Groups, no matter how inauspiciously they are formed, demand a format and focus, and Dark Grove was no exception. Tom, the oldest of them by several decades and trained in coven-craft, was the obvious leader, but tradition called for a partner to the priest and the title landed on Meredith. Meredith would be the acting High Priestess to Tom's High Priest and the coven's Seer.

"But what do we do, exactly?" asked Meredith one afternoon a week after the decision to form a coven and her naming as High Priestess. She and Tom sat on his deck watching deer wander into the back field, no doubt drawn to the area because of the promise of field corn to come and the natural spring in the copse of cedars beyond.

"We continue to learn and to grow in power. We honor and worship the Old Gods, we support each other."

"So, we're a church."

"No," he laughed, the sound deep and rumbling within his chest. "We are definitely not a church. You and I facilitate and guide the others so they can, in turn, facilitate others in the Craft."

"What makes us qualified to do that, Tom?"

"The Gods. Spirit. The Goddess. We only answer the call."

Meredith sipped at her tea and mulled over the conversation. In her mind, Tom's answers seemed vague and designed to absolve them of accountability. While she wasn't raised in a family that was, in any way, active in organized religion, her parents were often in leadership positions for charities or business ventures. She recognized the responsibility inherent within the role of 'leader.'

"You're concerned," said the older man.

"I am. Or confused, or maybe both," she replied.

"It's best not to overthink, Meredith. We're just a group of like-minded people who want to grow in power to help others in our community. We're limiting the number of people who can formally join the coven because only the strongest are cut out for inner court work. Some people are just better suited to participating in the outer court."

As Tom stood and walked back into the house to refresh his iced tea, Meredith couldn't help but feel a certain amount of pride. Not everyone was cut out to be an inner member of the coven, but she was. Despite her initial misgivings, she was interested to see how their group would grow.

As she sat watching the deer in the field and listening to the calling of the crows in the trees overhead, Tom stood inside, watching her. He wondered; would she be up to the task?

He left the large picture window that looked over the fields behind his house and walked down the hallway to his office. Tom had officially retired from his job as an accountant but kept his home office as his refuge and sanctuary. Within the darkly paneled room stood a handsome oak desk, several bookcases, and a huge curio cabinet that held all manner of oddities—some of which he had collected or found over the years and some that had been acquired by his father.

From within the depths of the top drawer of his desk, Tom located a small skeleton key, which he used to unlock the cabinet. He reached behind a reproduction of a shrunken head, terrifying in its realism, moved aside a small bowl of animal bones arranged around a black candle, and located the box hidden in the far back. The box seemed to not fit in with the more exotic and macabre items within the display case. It was neither terribly large nor interestingly small, there were no carvings or decorations upon its lid or sides, and the wood was a plain species, well-seasoned.

Holding the box with both hands as if it were made of fragile bone china or delicate glass, he took it to his desk and sat it down on the blotter. There was a keyhole but no key, and as far as he knew, there had never been one. His father, having returned with the box from a trip to New Orleans when Tom was just seven, had sat for hours staring at it. Occasionally he would reach out to touch it, then pull his finger back as if burned. Even at his young age, Tom was well-versed in his father's eccentricities and saw his obsession with the wooden box as just another aspect of what made his father so odd.

When Tom was thirteen years old, his father called him into his room. There sat the box, resting on the plaid duvet, an obsession in its physical form.

"Tom, come here. Sit down next to me, son."

Tom sat next to his father, the mattress bending to his body weight.

"Close your eyes. Can you see the box?"

Tom did as he was asked.

"Yes, I can see the box," he answered in a whisper. Pleasing his father was important to him, but still fraught with hidden dangers.

"Good, good! Now, I want you to try to open that box—the one you can see with your eyes shut. Can you do that?"

Tom's father sounded absolutely delighted. Tom should have felt happy, but he was quite terrified. There was a brittle note to his father's delight, like a goblet that is apt to shatter when rung too forcibly by a butter knife at a fancy dinner.

Tom sat motionless. In his mind's eye, he observed the box. It was deceptively dull, but when viewed in this manner, waves of sickly green floated out from the spaces where the wood didn't seam together tightly. He didn't want to touch it, let alone open it, and he was old enough to quickly weigh the potential of danger from one point to another. His father was mercurial in his responses, just as easily delighted as enraged. The box seemed to have no inherent goodness, emanating a steady stream of slick illness.

"I'm sorry, I can't open it," said Tom as he opened his eyes. He had made his choice and would take his chances with his father's erratic moods.

"Did you even try?" his father yelled as Tom stood and moved away from the man who had begun to work himself into a fury.

"Yes! I tried, but I just don't know how. I'm sorry!" Tom lied, with no weight of guilt. Living with his father put survival and safety as the highest priorities, and that often meant lying. Tom had become very good at it.

Truthfully, he hadn't tried to open the box. He couldn't tell what lay within, and that frightened him a great deal. He vowed that he would not open the box until he knew what it contained.

Over the years, his father repeated his request that Tom visualize the box and then attempt to open it from that inner state. He never asked his son to physically open it. This bit of strangeness from an already strange man made Tom even more certain that he should not open the box until he knew what it held.

Tom's father passed away in his sleep, an oddly peaceful and mundane death for a man who lived on the edge of sanity for most of his life. When the family home was cleaned out and put up for sale, Tom rented a storage locker close to his own home in Horton Bay and stored the few items that he chose to keep. Some were sentimental, some had a bit of monetary value, and others had practical uses. But the box from New Orleans he brought home and placed into the curio cabinet in his office.

It wasn't lost on him that his father's obsession with the object had transferred to him. He had even briefly thought of dumping the thing into Lake Charlevoix, but he couldn't bring himself to do it. Over the years, in his quest to understand the cursed thing, Tom joined esoteric groups and attended psychic gatherings, and in these pursuits, he gained immense knowledge but little insight. Then he met Meredith. Young, untrained, and the most powerful Seer he had ever met, he hoped that she would be able to solve the mystery once and for all. But before that, he needed to ensure that a strong group, well-versed in the arts of the Craft, stood around her. While he desperately wanted to know what the box contained, he was also terribly afraid of whatever it might be.

Chapter 11

The sun shone brightly down on the large lawn that spread out from the back of Tom's house and was framed with the dense green of the corn. Meredith looked around at her coven mates, more like family than she had ever thought possible when she attended Tom's burgeoning study group almost two years prior. With her help, he had picked the core group, the inner court, that would become the working coven. The others that were best suited for attending holiday gatherings or rite of passage rituals such as hand-fastings or baby blessings remained in the outer court. Contrary to what Meredith had always heard about witches and their groups, there was no need for any certain number. Their coven was made up of just seven: herself, Tom, Camryn, Riley, Micheal, and a married couple—Rose and Nathan. They worked well together, and Meredith trusted each of them, though she was more friendly with Riley than any of the others.

"What are you thinking about?"

Tom's always-outdoor-voice broke into her silent reverie. Tamping down her annoyance at being startled, something she suspected that he did on purpose, Meredith turned and looked up at her friend that stood head and shoulders above her already tall frame.

"Just watching them set the altar. I like the addition of the sunflowers."

Tom glanced over her shoulder to watch Riley place the coven's chalice, athame, ritual candles, and the rest of the elemental accouterments in their traditional places on the altar. The vase containing seasonal flowers at the far back made a lovely focal point.

"She does a nice job with the altar. Will you have her open it with the blessing, or will you do that this time?"

Meredith smiled, "I'll be doing it today."

Tom watched as the statuesque young woman squared her shoulders and adjusted the cord that hung around her waist, its bright red color contrasting with the black of her robe. He smiled at how easily she had stepped into the role of High Priestess, though she rarely used the title. Meredith referred to herself as an agnostic and was more comfortable with the title of 'group leader,' but Tom liked the tradition of High Priest and, therefore, he insisted on her assuming the title of High Priestess. Tom allowed for an 'equal partnership' between him and Meredith when it suited him.

"Happy Midsummer," Riley smiled as Meredith approached.

"Happy Midsummer," replied Meredith as she held her hand out for the lighter that Riley held.

Riley handed it over, never sure when Meredith would choose to bless and open the altar, but knowing it was within her power to do so.

Meredith often felt cold and unattached to the religious end of their group gatherings, firmly holding to her position as an agnostic Witch. There had been many intense—though not unfriendly—discussions and debates about whether this was even possible, with all sides having interesting and compelling arguments on the matter. Meredith didn't care; in her way of thinking, the Craft was a set of skills that utilized energy. It was science. The Gods? Maybe they existed, and maybe not. If they had a personal relationship with humans, Meredith hadn't yet seen it. She accepted that Gods and Goddesses could be personifications of energy, but those attributes were assigned by humans which didn't make the Gods sentient, it made them mirrors for those who called upon them.

But energy and its movement to affect change or a desired outcome? That was something that Meredith believed in and excelled at. This was a skill, and she had set out to become the best. All of this was not to say that she discounted other entities—ghosts, elementals, fairies, or familiars, all of which she understood as being a part of the multifaceted world in which she lived. But divine entities worthy of worship or adoration? No, she couldn't get her heart or head around the concept. She realized that she had been standing lost in her thoughts and hoped that the coven members who gathered would think she was meditating and preparing for the beginning of the ritual.

Meredith closed her eyes and held both of her arms over the altar, palms down. She could feel the energy of the ritual items, a slow pulsing of both innate and embedded vibrations held within each. The vase of flowers radiated their own energetic pattern, as vibrant and bright as the summer sun that they represented.

Opening her eyes, she steadied herself and allowed the group standing just outside her field of vision to drop away from her consciousness.

"Creature of Fire, Work Your Will At My Desire." She lit the small red taper that sat at the southernmost quadrant of the altar and began chanting the words that would gather the energies for her work.

Taking a deep breath, Meredith continued with the consecration ritual. She raised her left hand over her head. With her right, she stirred the wisps that swirled about the elements and ritual tools in a slow sensuous movement, blending their essences so they became a cohesive unit gathered together to perform a specific rite. Meredith saw this as a metaphor for the group as a whole, and at this point in the consecration, moved her consciousness back out to encompass the humans gathered there so that they, too, would form a unified group working together for a desired outcome.

After having moved the energies clockwise three times, Meredith took a deep breath and began intoning the final invocation, "Honor Is The Law—Love Is The Bond, Honor Is The Law—Love Is The Bond."

Over and over she chanted, moving and blending the energies of the altar, chanting faster as she felt the magic swirling up and up in a cone over her head. At the peak, she rapped the edge of the altar three times, stomped her foot to ground the excess vibrations, and felt the bright magic settle back onto the altar, draping it like a shimmering silken shawl.

At the stomp of her foot, the others gathered and formed a semi-circle around her as Tom took up his place to her right. Riley, with a nod of assent from Meredith, cast the magic circle around those gathered, sealing their working within until the group was ready to release their intentions out into the world.

The gathering of the Dark Grove Coven began its Midsummer ritual to celebrate abundance, blessings, and growth.

Chapter 12

Outside of the large windows of the living room it was cold and gray, and the autumn waves of Lake Michigan crashed at the shoreline below the cliff upon which her home sat. It had taken a bit of settling in, but Meredith truly felt that she was the rightful Mistress of Rosehaven now, rather than an intruder within her mother's domain.

Her place within Dark Grove Coven had also felt more genuine, despite the ongoing push and pull of focus for the group. Tom seemed entirely dedicated to acquiring and maintaining power, while Meredith was more interested in group cohesiveness and well-being. Most times they were able to reach a mutually agreed upon neutral ground with Meredith acknowledging that empowering the group and its members was the first step in their working toward their well-being. Tom's approach, however, remained far more militant than her own, which Meredith chalked up to differences in their personalities.

Meredith's decision to not tell Dark Grove about her owl still confused her, but the feeling was so pervasive that they could not know that she remained silent. That's not to say that she ignored the owl. Far from it. Despite her disagreements with Tom about acquiring power for power's sake, she absolutely recognized it and didn't often shy away from it—certainly not when it was perched on her shoulder.

She enjoyed working with the owl and spent a good many of her afternoons learning what it was to her, how it could benefit her, and honing the skills necessary to summon it, direct it, and call it back to her.

After having sent the bird of prey out to overlook her coven mates (Rose and Nathan fought a lot more than she would have suspected, and Camryn liked to play the slots at the local casino), Meredith decided to ask it about something in the past.

"Show me my parents," she whispered, her eyes closed and her body relaxed. She had found that staying just this side of a full meditation garnered her the best results, as well as asking questions that were open-ended and vague.

Meredith felt the change in pressure as the bird of prey took to the ether. Sometimes she sat, half awake and half in a trance, for up to an hour before she felt its return, and sometimes only a minute or two. This time, the owl returned to her after just a few minutes. She felt the pressure deepen as it settled in and then the images began playing behind her eyelids like a movie with little context.

She saw her mother at college—happy, popular, and engaging. Then her father, a studious and careful college student more comfortable with numbers than people. The images tumbled past her eyes so fast that she gave up trying to see what each was until suddenly they stopped. She saw her mother and father in a shabby apartment, joyfully putting together a baby's crib, only for the scene to be replaced with a still of her mother sobbing on a bloodstained bathroom floor.

"These are images of their past," she said aloud as Eliza began her frantic movements overhead.

"*All times are now,*" whispered a voice in her head. It had no inflection, no discernible gender, and yet was not robotic. Meredith wasn't afraid of the voice but curious as to what, or who, it was. She had heard it before when working with her owl but couldn't be sure if it was the owl's voice or another spirit's.

"All times are now," she mulled over how this information could help her.

"Show me, then, what I need to know now," she said to the owl.

The bird regarded its Mistress with cold eyes, before breaking the gaze with a slow blink and turning its head almost ninety degrees to the right. It lifted itself up and away, gliding through the walls that separated it from the outside, and banked to the left as it rode the thermal currents over the trees and into the mists over the lake.

Meredith sat and waited as she maintained her semi-conscious state and kept her mind as blank as possible.

She wasn't sure how long the owl was gone or if she had, perhaps, fallen asleep. At some point, a series of images assaulted her brain of a child that shone so brightly that it was, at first, difficult to see its features.

Breathing deeply to calm the anxiety that the immense light produced, Meredith steadied herself enough to see clearly the person behind the brilliant glow.

True to its statement that all time is now, the images that the owl showed her were a jumble of times, places, and ages of the Bright One, and Meredith could only ascertain that each image was the same girl, despite the age or place, because of her red hair.

She saw a toddler swaddled in a hand-knit blanket crying in what appeared to be a home office. A school-aged redhead, shy and alone, wandering the trails in a pine wood. A young girl of about ten years sitting on the bottom-most mattress of a shabby bunk bed, clutching the same hand-knit blanket and crying silently. It was, perhaps, the saddest vision Meredith had seen to date. But through it all, the Light of the redhead shone brightly, neither extinguished nor dampened by her circumstances.

Meredith's eyes fluttered and opened, her breathing both shallow and rapid.

"Why have you shown me this girl?"

The owl, having returned to perch on her shoulder during the cascading visions it provided, only blinked.

"Who is she? What is that light? I've never seen that around anyone before. It's so much more than an aura," continued Meredith while the owl watched her. "Why do I need to know about this child?"

Still, the owl remained mute.

Frustrated, Meredith uncrossed her legs and stood up, shaking the pins and needles from them one at a time, and felt the owl settle within her breast—its preferred place in between Meredith's summonings. She left the living room, crossed the main foyer, and entered the kitchen through the butler's pantry. Absentmindedly munching on a handful of almonds from the container on the counter, she ran the images through her mind slowly to get a better idea of the background.

"Where and when is this child?" she asked around a mouthful of nuts.

There was nary a flutter or a whisper from the owl.

"I asked you to show me what I need to know *now*. Does that mean that she's part of the present? Is she still a child right now?"

Suddenly, Meredith felt the immense bird move away from her and take flight. It was abrupt and without warning, and she nearly choked on the almonds that she was eating.

Dropping into the closest chair at the long kitchen table, she barely had time to swallow what was in her mouth before she fell into a trance so deep that she felt like Alice falling down the rabbit hole.

The first thing that Meredith noticed was that the air was humid and heavy, almost tropical. She certainly wasn't in Northern Michigan any longer. The next was that her center of gravity felt different, and her body seemed to be made up entirely of her chest, which was thick and without breasts. Her eyesight was incredibly sharp and her neck felt like a rubber band, allowing her head to swivel in an unfathomable way. Stretching her arms resulted in large feathered wings that spread out above her, and she let out a cry of surprise that sounded like the screech of an angry Banshee.

"I'm the owl?" her thoughts were still coherent and inherently human, but her voice produced the sounds of the night forest.

A bright light assailed her sharp eyesight, and she looked down from her perch which seemed to be a large lime tree. The redhead, who shone so brightly as a child, walked down the sidewalk below her as a young adult. Meredith felt her eyes blink in the slow way of the owl as the redhead ambled down the cracked sidewalk of the tropical urban neighborhood, seemingly happy, content, and incredibly strong.

Meredith dropped with a stomach-lurching fall into her own body and sat breathing rapidly.

"What the hell was that?" she cried, both exhilarated and terrified by the experience.

She could see the owl sitting in the Ficus tree between the kitchen and sunroom, its golden eyes regarding her with interest.

"So, you can go and find me information, and I can *be* you while this is happening?" Meredith asked the bird in a rush of loudly hysterical words.

"*Either or, and as you wish,*" said the methodical voice in her head as the owl took flight, flew twice around the kitchen, and settled back within her body.

Chapter 13

Ashlynne Barrow was a happy, if not somewhat shy, child. She loved her adopted father and godmother, and she thrived within the small island community of Saint James. She had no memories of her life before the parsonage and never questioned the story that her parents, kin to Father Greene, had died in a car accident in Kansas when she was just two years old. And for their part, the islanders—though they had never heard of Father Greene having relatives in Kansas—were all too happy to welcome the pretty redheaded child to their community without question.

Ashlynne spent most of her days playing in the gardens and yard of the parsonage.

What had previously been Father Greene's office was transformed into a simple, comfortable bedroom for Ashlynne. In the warmer months, however, the young girl was most often found outdoors.

Father Greene stood at the kitchen sink doing the lunch dishes and watching Ashlynne out of the window that looked out over the backyard. A small kitchen garden had been installed some years back and marginally maintained each season, depending on Father Greene's interest and time. This year he'd felt particularly motivated. Ashlynne, at five years old, was at that perfect age to help plant seeds and water the tidy rows of radishes, lettuce, carrots, and marigolds. The rose bushes that lined the southern edge of the garden plot didn't require much these days; by his reckoning, they must all be over thirty years old by now. He pruned them back every year and fed them regularly, and they responded with an assortment of glorious blooms in all shades of pink and red. Ashlynne, for her part, walked along the line of thorny bushes every afternoon and talked to each. Or at least he thought that was what she was doing. As he dried the lunch plates, he watched as she sat the small watering can down and, as was her habit, walked to the roses. Bending over each plant, she whispered, clapped her small hands together, and then moved on to the next in the row. Occasionally, she would let out a peel of laughter that never failed to bring a smile to his face.

Father Greene would have loved to know what she said to the flowers, and he had asked her on more than one occasion, but the child just giggled and provided no other information.

Ashlynne knew that her Papa was watching her out of the kitchen window as she watered the garden. This was her job every day after lunch. She and Papa would eat together in the kitchen—him a tuna salad sandwich and her a peanut butter and jam cut into four triangles. They usually had some fruit and a glass of lemonade or cocoa if it was chilly. When they finished eating, he would gather up the lunch plates, fill her pretty yellow watering can half full of water, and scoot her out the back door.

"Go to work, young lady!" he had said, trying to sound stern, but he could never hide the smile in his voice. Ashlynne loved having a job and took it very seriously. Not only did she love to water the plants, but she was able to say hello to the nice ladies that stood along the edge of her garden. Each woman wore a beautiful gown and a perfume that made Ashlynne's nose twitch. Their gowns were not just pink or red but had trims of variegated greens that deepened into brown. Ashlynne had tried to color with these hues one rainy day when she was set loose with her crayons and craft paper, but she couldn't get it right.

The row of beautifully dressed ladies always waved hello to her and smiled when she came over, but she knew not to ever touch them. All along the trimmings of their dresses poked spiky thorns that would draw blood. Ashlynne asked them one time why they had such hurtful things attached to such beautiful clothing, but they just smiled at her and nodded their heads drowsily under the warmth of the midday sunshine.

"Hi!" whispered Ashlynne, standing over the row of Rose Ladies.

"Hello, darling! How are you today?" answered the one wearing a gown of the deepest coral.

Ashlynne giggled, "I'm fine, thank you!" They had taught her how to respond as a proper young lady should, and the little girl was always careful to use 'please' and 'thank you' with them.

"Bright One, what is that bit of smudge on your lip, just there?" asked the Rose who wore the darkest of dark red gowns. Ashlynne thought maybe she was in charge, since the others always nodded in agreement with whatever she said.

The murmuring of the others began—a background of consensus that Ashlynne did, indeed, have a smudge of something on her lip.

"It's peanut butter, silly," whispered Ashlynne to the darkest of dark red Roses with a quiet giggle. "Don't you know what peanut butter is?"

"I'm afraid not, dearest," demurred the smallest of the Roses who was bedecked in the palest of pinks.

"We don't eat food like you do."

"Well, what do you eat then?" asked Ashlynne, whispering still in case Papa came out. No one had told her that they could or couldn't see the Roses, but she had a good idea that they couldn't see them like she could.

"We enjoy all kinds of tiny vitamins that you can't see," smiled the light pink Rose.

"Nitrogen, magnesium, potassium, and so many other wonderful things," sighed the magenta Rose.

"Ahhhh, and don't forget the glorious sunshine and long drinks of summer rain," said the Rose, whose color was as red as a stop sign.

"But I can water you! You don't have to wait for rain," whispered Ashlynne to the row of Roses.

"Sweet girl, of course you can, and if we need you to help us along, we'll whisper it to you when you visit. But we much prefer the lovely rain water for our summer soirees," laughed the deep red Rose.

"What's a soiree?" whispered Ashlynne.

"Why, it's a party!" laughed the pink, magenta, and dark red Roses as one.

"You have parties without me?" asked Ashlynne in a voice thick with hurt. She was, after all, only five. At five, friends always invite friends to their parties.

"Bright One, our garden parties are held in the rain, and you play inside on rainy days, yes?" asked the pale pink Rose.

"Yes," whispered Ashlynne, her eyes downcast.

"You may join us anytime, Ashlynne. Wear your raincoat and rubber boots and you will be fine," smiled the dark red Rose.

"OK," whispered Ashlynne to the Roses.

"I have to go now. Papa will be out soon."

"Bye, Ashlynne! Goodbye, sweet girl! We shall see you tomorrow!" The chorus of goodbyes and farewells and well-wishes sounded like the winds through the maple leaves and the gentle rolling of the lake a few miles away to all but the redheaded girl, who shone brightly as the sun.

Ashlynne stepped into the back door, took off her sandals that were full of garden dirt, and put her watering can on the kitchen counter.

"Papa! I'm inside now! I watered the garden!"

She padded barefooted through the kitchen and into the small living room as she continued to call out. Her voice bounced off of the parsonage walls, ricocheting back to her in the strangely quiet house.

"Papa?"

Ashlynne stood very still. There was no sense of her Papa in the house, and she hadn't heard the car start up. In fact, she couldn't feel him anywhere—not here, not out in the yard, and even though she stretched her thoughts out as far as she could, she couldn't feel him in the small grocery store that they always visited. Besides, he would never just get in the car and leave her here alone.

"Papa! Papa, where are you?" Ashlynne began to cry because if she couldn't feel him, then he was gone. Even at just five years old, she knew that if he was gone, then she was all alone.

Ashlynne found Father Green half on and half off of the small front porch. His eyes were closed and his face relaxed. At first, she thought maybe he was just asleep. But in her heart of hearts, she knew that he would never just lie down on the steps and fall asleep.

"Papa?" she whispered.

The rustle of the trees and the sharp call of the blue jays were her only answer.

Ashlynne returned to the kitchen and dragged a chair from the table where they had had lunch not even an hour ago to the phone that hung on the wall. She lifted the receiver and dialed the number that she had been taught to call 'in an emergency.' While an 'emergency' had never really been defined, she guessed this was one, and so she did as her Papa had instructed her.

"Hello," she whispered into the receiver, "this is Ashlynne Borrow, and I think my Papa is sick."

She replaced the receiver and went outside to sit next to the man who was the only father she had ever known.

As the ambulance screeched and wailed its way up the road and into the driveway of the parsonage, the Roses began their keening on behalf of the small child that they had become so fond of.

Chapter 14

Ashlynne sat on the plastic-covered mattress of the bottom bunk and clutched the yellow and purple afghan to her chest, a black plastic garbage bag wedged between her feet. The last wisps of her Papa's cologne laced itself around her head, just barely covering the smells of plastic, pine-scented cleanser, and last night's meatloaf.

She had been taken to her godmother's house after her Papa died but, at almost eighty years old, Mrs. Boyle's family thought that taking care of a five-year-old was just too much for her, and the county's social services had been contacted to find other arrangements.

'Other arrangements' meant foster care, and while it took most of the rest of the summer to finalize it all, Ashlynne would start school on the mainland. This was the first time in her memory to be off of Beaver Island and away from the people she knew and loved.

The yelling and screaming of other children pulled Ashlynne from her thoughts and back into the dormitory-style room in which she now resided. Though the noises had startled her, she could tell that it was only kids at play and nothing to be worried about, at least for now. Ashlynne had never felt so alone as she did now, so everything seemed worrisome and scary. Though she could feel the different moods and vibrations that flowed through the group home, and that gave her a bit more of a safety net as far as how to proceed and who to trust. For now, the little girl decided to trust no one and just watch.

The redhead wasn't the only one observing. The owl sat outside the group home, watching Ashlynne through the second-floor window from its perch within a large pine tree next to the building. It watched as she was led in by an older child and shown to her bunk. It watched as she wrinkled her nose against the smells of old cooking, plastic, and harsh cleansers. It watched as she sat down on the mattress—bare except for a yellowed waterproof covering—and clutched the afghan from her home to her chest. The owl watched as the brilliant light that played out around and about her shone as brightly as it ever had, and then it took flight out of the tree and back over the farms and forests of Northern Lower Michigan to return to its Mistress at Rosehaven.

Meredith felt the pressure as her owl settled back into her chest and the images played out behind her closed eyelids.

"Is this happening now?" she asked about the now-familiar scene as she sat up and reached for her glass of iced tea.

The voice that she had come to associate with her owl replied, "The images shown are of the child as she is within your present time. She resides on the Island called Beaver no longer. She is on the mainland, just as you are."

Meredith sipped her tea and considered what needed to be done. Her owl had already shown her disjointed pieces and parts of this girl's life. She had pieced together a tentative timeline, so she knew that, at some point, the girl would move south. What she couldn't yet understand was why the owl had shown her this young girl, to begin with. Was she supposed to become a part of the coven? Did she have something to do with her parents, who were often on Beaver Island? Meredith understood that Ashlynne was, most certainly, a special girl. She had never seen

Light like that around another human, but what that had to do with Meredith remained a mystery.

The car horn beeping from outside jolted Meredith from her thoughts, and she glanced at her wrist. "Early," she muttered in annoyance. Over the years, Meredith had become self-contained and strong. She felt certain that when she gave instructions about how, when, or why something should be done, those instructions would be followed.

She stood, smoothed her dress, and slipped her feet into the black stiletto heels that completed her outfit.

"Goodbye for a bit!" she called out to Eliza as she opened the service door, bumping her wheeled carry-on bag behind her and plastering a smile onto her face so that Riley wouldn't see her annoyance.

"Sorry I'm early," said Riley with a smile as Meredith slid into the front seat, pulling her sunglasses from her bag.

"It's OK," she lied easily as the white Subaru pulled out of the driveway and began the first leg of Meredith's long trip.

"Aren't you excited to be going to Scotland?" asked Riley, her envy slipping through despite her attempts to hide it.

"I am, though I'll be more excited when I get to O'Hare," laughed Meredith. She mentally calculated her time from the small airport in Traverse City to the larger airport in Chicago that would eventually deposit her in Edinburgh. This far north, there were no direct flights, but flying business class would help to lessen the inconvenience of the long trip.

Meredith sat back and let her friend's endless chattering lull her to an almost sleep state. She had finally felt strong enough to leave Rosehaven and travel, as had been suggested by her parents' lawyers from almost the first day of the accident that changed everything. She had resisted citing school, then repairs and upgrades on the house, and then because of her duties to Dark Grove Coven. It was Tom who finally convinced her to take a much-needed trip and even suggested that she see Scotland—a place she had never been to, so it would be devoid of painful memories.

"You can start fresh, as your own person!" he boomed at her across the table of the bar where they had met to discuss upcoming plans for the group and enjoy a beer.

She smiled at the memory and wondered why it had taken Tom's suggestion of travel to loosen her ties to her house, even for a short time.

"When do you come home again? I can't remember."

Riley's question broke through her thoughts and she replied with a smile, "September. I'm taking the whole summer."

"The whole summer! Who will watch the house?"

"I have housekeepers that visit, and Tom said that he would stop over now and then to check on things."

Riley smiled over at Meredith. "That's great. I hope you have a wonderful time."

"I think it will be just what I've needed," Meredith smiled back.

Chapter 15

Meredith curled up on the tartan loveseat that sat under the large window of her room. The view, blurred by the filmy off-white sheers, highlighted the bustle and medieval grandeur of Princes Street in Edinburgh.

Stretching, she swung her legs off the small sofa and padded across the room to the coffee bar for a warm-up on her midday indulgence. Normally she wouldn't drink so much caffeine so late in the day, but there was a late night ahead, and she needed the extra jolt of energy. She was still groggy and muzzy-headed after her nap earlier.

Adding a drop of heavy cream to the dark brew in her cup, Meredith considered her last few weeks in Scotland. She had booked rooms for the summer at the Balmoral on Princes Street and had not one regret given the price tag associated with her accommodations. The decor maintained a traditional feel, very much like her own Rosehaven, but with little splashes of modern European art here and there. The service was divine, with her room being serviced at a standard two times per day unless she dictated otherwise. Her bathroom could only be described as decadent—resplendent as it was with Italian marble, burnished brass fixtures, and luxurious linens. The skincare and bath products provided were simply to die for. Meredith felt pampered and taken care of from the minute she stepped into the cavernous yet quiet lobby; a vision in marble, potted palms, and crystal.

Meredith smiled. To think that she felt perfectly at home amongst this quiet elegance, but her parents, had they been alive, would be aghast at her choice of hotel and the cost associated with it. Meredith, having successfully navigated the years since their deaths, the lawyers for the estate, and the myriad other bits and pieces of what they had left behind, had discovered that with shrewd investments and acquisitions to the existing stock portfolios, she had not only enough money to live more than comfortably for the remainder of her own life but her children's as well, should she choose to have any. Armed with that knowledge, she chose to indulge herself here and there and this summer was an extravagance that had been planned and allocated for by attorneys and advisers alike. Meredith had never been a fool, and knowing the amount of her personal wealth didn't change that.

She finished her final cup of coffee, consulted the menu for room service, and called in her preference. It would take at least forty-five minutes for her dinner to arrive, so she would take her shower now. The server could let themselves in with her food if it was ready before she was out of the bathroom.

The invigorating shower and the cheese and fruit tray did as much to perk her up as the coffee, and Meredith felt alert and ready for just about anything as she walked down Princes Street, meandering at a leisurely pace through Old Town until she reached the Neo-Gothic extravagance known as the Hub. Crossing the Royal Mile, Meredith walked past shops selling tartans and woolens, ancient-looking pubs, and an eatery proclaiming 'Proper Fish and Chips!' The smell of fried fish and potatoes and the tang of vinegar made her stomach rumble, though she wasn't at all hungry.

"I need to stop and eat there before I leave," she muttered to herself for the millionth time since she had first passed by the small restaurant weeks ago.

Taking the next left turn into Saint James Close, Meredith slowed her pace as the ancient walls moved in on her. The darkness tunneled her vision to the only brightness available—the opening to the courtyard at the end of the tunnel of seventeenth-century stonework.

When she had first arrived in the city, the dark warrens had scared her, leaving her less than enthusiastic about the idea of exploring them. However, deciding to play tourist one afternoon, she joined a walking tour and was led down one narrow close, or alley, after another until she realized that the majority of them were simply walkways to apartments or the University of Edinburgh residence halls.

Meredith replaced her sunglasses, removed in the gloom of the close, as she emerged into the courtyard. It was stunningly quiet, which never failed to impress her. The noise of trolleys, trams, and cars was so muffled by the ancient stone buildings that they almost didn't exist, making it evident why the upper classes of the past had moved into these towering tenements rather than staying on the main roadways and walking paths of the old city.

Checking her watch, Meredith saw that she wasn't as late as she had feared, but rather, a few minutes early. She sat on one of the many cement benches scattered about the central fountain to catch her breath and wait for her appointment.

Within no time it seemed, the relative quiet of the secluded courtyard was broken by the shrill trilling of Chloe Bathgate.

"Meredith! You're here! Come, come — let's go inside out of this unbearable heat!"

Chloe, dressed in so many layers of assorted black and gauze wraps and shawls that the frigid wind and rain of early February would be felt as 'unbearably' hot, linked her arm with Meredith's and hauled her up from the bench in one smooth motion, all the while chattering on like a magpie that had been given too much sugar.

Meredith tripped along and was dragged into the vestibule of the middle apartment before her arm was released, and Chloe stopped talking long enough to envelop her in a sage and patchouli-scented embrace.

"Darling," trilled the older woman holding Meredith at arm's length, "it's so good to see you!"

"It's been exactly one week, Chloe, but it's good to know you haven't lost your flair for the dramatic in the last seven days!" laughed Meredith.

Chloe laughed and led Meredith up the stairs to her third-floor flat, still chattering and going on about the past week and customers who came into the shop that were either troublesome, endearing, or outright thieves.

Chloe's shop, the Witchery, was where the two had met. Shortly after arriving in the city,

Meredith decided to wander on her own without a map and was hopelessly lost within the hour. Having made one too many wrong turns, she finally gave up as the sun set. She went into the next available shop with its windows lit and its 'open' sign on. The fact that an assortment of spell books and handcrafted broomsticks were prominently displayed in one window just served to seal the deal for her.

Not only did Chloe draw her a perfectly serviceable map that would take her back to the Balmoral, but she invited her for dinner and drinks around the corner from her shop before Meredith set off for her rooms. By the end of their dinner, Chloe had divulged that she owned and ran the Witchery but was an initiate of a British Traditional Wiccan group, and a weekly study had been set up between the two women.

"Kismet!" cried Chloe as she ushered Meredith into the front room and closed the door behind them, locking it for good measure.

"It certainly was!" responded Meredith with a laugh.

"What? What certainly was?" asked Chloe, who was unwinding her wraps like a mummy in the throes of a fever.

"Our meeting," replied Meredith, watching the older woman toss yards of gray and black fabric across a delicate Louis XIV chair.

"Oh, yes. Certainly, it was! But I was talking about my new fish. His name is Kismet!"

Meredith peered into the large round fish bowl that Chloe indicated and watched as the fattest black goldfish she had ever seen swam in energetic circles about the perimeter.

"Why is it upside down?" she asked, looking over her shoulder at Chloe, who was lighting sticks of incense.

"He's a *he,* and it's just a bit of a problem with his swim bladder. That's all."

Meredith watched as Kismet's googly eyes wandered side to side as he valiantly traversed his bowl with his fat belly positioned at the top of the water's edge.

"Is that all, then? Well, he sure is determined, isn't he?"

Moving away from the folly of the upside-down fish, Meredith slid off her sandals and curled her feet under her on Chloe's sofa, which had seen better days. The decor of the small apartment was equal parts high-end French antique and found-it-on-the-curb chic. Strangely enough, it all seemed to work together, and Meredith marveled anew at her friend's innate sense of style. She wanted to know more about how it had developed, but Chloe became guarded and close-mouthed when Meredith asked anything about her past or how she came to be in Edinburgh. She didn't have a Scottish accent. In fact, she didn't have much of a specific accent at all, just a way of speaking that seemed to be generically European.

"What's that?" asked Meredith as Chloe held her hand out toward her.

"This, Meredith, is a Journey Stone," proclaimed Chloe with a dramatic flourish that didn't seem to go with the smooth and mostly nondescript stone that she held in the palm of her hand. In fact, except for the bright white band of quartz running around the outside edge, there was absolutely nothing special about the stone at all.

Chloe laughed a genuine deep belly laugh when Meredith said as much and wiping tears of amusement from her eyes replied, "My dear, this stone can move you, that chair, or my Kismet from where they currently are to where you would like them to be. It's very astounding."

"Is it hard to learn?"

"Of course it is," laughed Chloe, "but isn't that true for most of the amazing things that we do?"

And so began what would become one of the most important lessons of Meredith's life as she and the indescribably flamboyant Chloe Bathgate began the intricate work of transferring a person or thing from their current position to another position entirely.

Chapter 16

Week after week, Meredith met with Chloe to train, discuss, and enjoy the company of someone with similar tastes and interests. Most often, they stayed in Chloe's apartment, but occasionally they would meet at a park or pub as the weather warmed and the sky stayed bright for longer.

"So, Tom began this coven based on his training, you say?" asked Chloe, sipping gingerly at the hot tea in her cup.

"Mhm," replied Meredith around a bite of biscuit that she had just popped into her mouth. Swallowing the sweet pastry, similar to what she would call a cookie in the United States, she took a sip of her tea and nodded.

"Yes, he is a Traditional Witch. When he finished his training, he wanted a group in our area to continue the work and celebrate the seasons and Sabbats."

Chloe, gazing off somewhere beyond Meredith's left shoulder, nodded and asked, "Trained by who, exactly? And within which tradition?"

"He trained under the guidance of Midnight Bluestone and her group called Blackstone Hearth, in the tradition of the Dark Tree Clan."

Chloe lifted one dark eyebrow as Meredith spouted out this memorized lineage of her High Priest.

"What?" asked Meredith, catching the dubious look that crossed the other woman's face.

"Do you know who Midnight Bluestone is, by chance?" asked Chloe.

"I know she heads up the Dark Tree Clan, and she's a well-known Pagan author, but I've never met her," replied Meredith, trying hard to not sound defensive and not sure why she felt that way to begin with. After all, Tom spoke so highly of her and based almost the entirety of their practice on her teachings.

"Ah, yes. *Well known.* She is certainly that," chuckled Chloe. "I carry several of her books in the shop and they are quite popular with the new-to-the-Craft set, but I've not seen many with Traditional Craft training clambering to snatch up any of the volumes."

"You don't approve of her?" asked Meredith, trying very hard to maintain a neutral tone.

"I think it's very easy for smart people to create a history that will attract talented people to further their own cause," replied Chloe, looking into her teacup rather than at Meredith.

"But you've said I have great skill—I learned that from my group!" protested Meredith.

Chloe studied the plate of sweets that sat between them and selected a small iced cake. Setting it next to her teacup, she finally looked up at her friend.

"Darling, you have always had these gifts, and your own practice sharpened your skills. I believe you have much more to offer Dark Grove Coven than they have to offer you."

Meredith squirmed and fought the emotions that battled within her. What Chloe suggested was that she, alone, was responsible for her strength, but that didn't line up with the feeling of power that occurred when her group worked as one. It was like being linked to an immense battery — thrilling, energizing, and powerful. Meredith seriously doubted she could gather that much energy alone and said as much to her friend.

"Meredith, I'm not saying that energy isn't gathered and used within your group. In fact, if your Tom has the training that he claims to have, then he should have been facilitating this all along and teaching you how to do it as well. It's basic priest craft. What I am saying is that not all groups are what they say they are or seem to be, especially groups that have a built-in hierarchy. The cagey Witch will balance what she is told by those in charge, against what her spirit tells her is so."

"But!" Meredith began, the raised hand from her friend and mentor silenced her.

"Yes, yes, I know. You are an agnostic Witch. You have told me this many times. Label yourself as you see fit, but the label will not change the fact—yes, fact—that as Witches, we move energy to effect a desired change. Spell craft 101. Spell craft 102 is that this begins on the inner or spiritual planes and if Witches traverse the spiritual planes, then they too must have a spirit. Trust that part of you that moves between the worlds, Meredith.

Meredith immediately thought of her owl but decided against telling Chloe about it. For an unknown reason, it seemed vitally important that she not let anyone know about this aspect of her Craft just yet.

"How have you been doing with the Journey Stone activities?" asked Chloe, anxious to jettison that topic and lighten the mood a bit. She had said her piece and warned the younger woman of the built-in perils of group minds that work with magic and felt it was now time to move on. Meredith would consider and heed her advice or not— it was not up to Chloe how the other woman should proceed.

"It's going well, though I'm not sure if I maybe added something to the process that I shouldn't have," replied Meredith with a smile. She, too, was happy to move on from the lecture on coven dynamics.

"Oh! How interesting. What have you added?" cried Chloe, clapping her hands in delight.

Meredith smiled, "Well, I'm not sure if it's right or appropriate, but come outside and I'll show you."

The two women cleaned up from their afternoon tea and made their way down the three flights of stairs to the courtyard below. Meredith extracted her own Journey Stone from her pocket—a gift from Chloe—and a small blown glass ball from her bag.

"I am so intrigued!" laughed Chloe, taking a seat on one of the stone benches.

Meredith looked around the courtyard until she saw what she was looking for—a squirrel scampered beneath one of the large trees, gathering this and that to bury and hide for times of scarcity.

Chloe followed Meredith's gaze to the squirrel and then looked back at her friend who stood motionless, the Journey Stone in one hand and the blown glass orb sitting just next to her on the ledge of the fountain.

Meredith planted her feet firmly onto the bricks of the courtyard and drew in a deep breath, feeling the rush of energy from the ground beneath enter her and settle at her diaphragm. Smiling slightly at the rush of it, she exhaled and felt her body grow heavy as if she had thrown thick roots from her feet into the earth below. Focusing on the tiny brown body several feet away from her, she raised the stone, whispered the words that Chloe had taught her, and pulled the energy of the small animal with all of her will into the stone. Then, with one fluid motion, she swung her arm around and threw that energy from the stone at the glass ball, creating an audible *crack* sound like that of a lightning strike.

"What has just happened?!" cried Chloe, jumping to her feet and running to the glass ball. "Where is the squirrel? Did you not send it to the fountain's ledge?" she asked, assuming that the glass bauble was set there as a point of focus.

Meredith smiled broadly and held the ball out to her friend. Chloe took it and fixed Meredith with a confused look.

"Hold it up and look inside, Chloe."

"Oh, my Gods! What have you done?" cried Chloe in alarm as the squirrel within the glass orb peered out at her.

"I told you, I added something to the practice."

"You've moved the squirrel *into* a vessel? How will it get out? Do you know how to do that?"

Meredith laughed as Chloe fired several questions at her in rapid succession.

"Of course! I experimented with bugs first, then moved on to larger animals. Since I was able to move a Saint Bernard into a teapot and back out again, I'm almost positive that I can move a human being next."

Chloe stared at the young woman with a mixture of admiration and trepidation.

"Meredith, why would you do this?"

"Why not?" asked Meredith as she reversed the spell and watched as the squirrel sat dazed and wide-eyed at their feet for several seconds before teetering off into the underbrush that surrounded the courtyard.

Chloe felt the chills roll up and down her back from the crown of her head to her toes as she tried to reconcile the pretty blonde woman she considered her friend with the coldly calculating Witch that stood before her. She wasn't sure any longer who should be concerned with who. Should Meredith be careful of Dark Grove Coven or should her coven be careful of her?

Chapter 17

The owl watched from an adjoining rooftop as Ashlynne hoisted her black garbage bag of belongings over one shoulder and stared at the large farmhouse in front of her. The wrap-around porch and steeply gabled roof should have sent out ripples of welcoming ribbons in shades of pink and lavender and light blue, but instead all Ashlynne—and the attending Owl—could see were waves of sickly green, dark red, and the deepest of blacks seen to date around any of the previous foster care homes. Ashlynne had seen more of those than she had thought possible. The owl saw all of this too and reported back to its Mistress, who seemed content to let the young girl traverse this particular road on her own for now without stepping in or changing the scenarios for the better.

"Observe. Do not, under any circumstance, intervene," declared Meredith, when the owl had shown her a particularly harrowing experience between Ashlynne and a man old enough to be her grandfather.

Ashlynne watched as the door opened and a tiny bird of a woman stood with one hand on her hip and the other waving her forward.

"Come on! We need to get you in and processed before dinner!" came the shrill voice.

Ashlynne cringed at both the ear-ringing tone and the word 'process' with all of its attending connotations; foster kids weren't welcomed, greeted, or introduced. They were processed. The experience was as cold and impersonal as the word sounded.

She looked over her shoulder for the sheriff's deputy who had driven her here but the car was already speeding back down the unpaved lane to the main highway, the clouds of dust from the late summer drought partially obscuring the van that had transported her here. Another coldly efficient word that was part of her world now, 'transport.' She wasn't 'given a ride' to a location, but transported like cattle or building supplies.

"Girl! You heard me! Come inside!"

Ashlynne trudged up the uneven and broken sidewalk toward the screeching woman and into the latest group home. If the colors emanating from the structure were any indication—and in Ashlynne's experience, they almost always were—this place would be truly hellish.

"It's about time!" snapped the woman, who had been screeching at her from the porch since the sheriff had dropped her at the end of the dirt road.

"I'm sorry," whispered Ashlynne, her face a

study in bland non-emotion. Stoicism was imperative to the young girl's survival over the last several years as she traversed the dystopian nightmare that had become her life. Gone were chats with the Roses in her Papa's garden. Gone were the laughter and bad jokes that flowed around their lunch table. Gone was the security and knowledge that she was loved and cared for. Most importantly, gone was the idea that she was safe. In her new life, she was not loved, not cared for, had no reason to laugh or joke, and was absolutely not safe.

This mask of blandness also made sure that whatever she saw would not be evident to the adults or older children in the home—people who had secrets to keep and would violently protect those secrets if they felt threatened or exposed.

As Ashlynne got closer, the woman hurrying her inside the house looked less like a bird and more like a winged fox. Her eyes were both slanted and sly, her nose more of an elongated snout than a beak, and the wings that sprouted from her back had feathers of gleaming orange tipped in black.

Ashlynne was still young, but she had learned that people who also looked like animals or monsters were never good news. She hadn't yet decided if these types were completely human whose monstrous acts gave them monster attributes or if they were completely monsters who played at being human to stay in this world.

Slipping past the winged fox lady and into the front hall, Ashlynne waited while her eyes adjusted to the darkness. She dearly wished to be back outside in the warm sunshine but knew from previous experience that unless there were gardens to work or yards to be maintained she would more than likely spend the majority of her days within the walls of the house washing clothes, cleaning bathrooms, or vacuuming rugs. In a world where very little could be counted on, Ashlynne knew, without fail, that foster kids were saddled with chores from daybreak to lights out when they weren't in school.

"Go on! Move!" said the house matron as she manhandled Ashlynne further into the house. Doors opened to her left and right along the length of the hallway—doors that were opened to rooms that showed the thin places that Ashlynne has come to dread. At each doorway, the air shimmered and swirled with the same dark reds and greens shot through with inky black that had flowed out from the house's exterior. As she walked past each, glimpses of other places and realities could be seen within, sickly forests, huge insects that rattled and clacked their appendages as they gorged themselves on platters of rotten fruit set out on banquet tables so long as to reach the horizon, and the small cottages on legs that she had seen at other thin spots that marched down cobbled paths to destinations unknown. Their windows filled with the flailing arms of those who were trapped within.

At the last door, before she was pushed into the kitchen, a tiny boy of only five or six years old stumbled out, his face awash with tears and terror. Behind him, a teenager with the head of a wolf grinned and slobbered, its tongue lolling out from between razor-sharp teeth.

Ashlynne had been within the walls of this house for exactly two and a half minutes, and she knew without a doubt that she would not be staying. As the winged fox woman droned on about house rules and the teenager with the wolf's head eyed her as potential prey, the redhead, with the uncanny ability to see and hear what others could not, plotted her escape.

The owl took flight, seeing all that it needed, and banked west toward the mists that allowed it to move between realms and back to its Mistress. It needed to report this new location to the Witch.

Sipping her tea at a sidewalk table outside of a small cafe close to the Balmoral, Meredith felt the heaviness within her solar plexus as the owl returned. She had opted to send it out separately from her own consciousness so she could enjoy the people-watching that had become a favorite pastime of hers.

She closed her eyes behind the large black sunglasses, so dark that anyone looking at her would be none the wiser, and watched as the owl played back the scenery of the journey from which it had just returned.

"She's growing stronger," she whispered as she watched Ashlynne's non-reaction to the horrors that unfolded along the hallway of the group home.

"So much atrocity, yet her Light shines just as bright as ever!" Meredith smiled at the vision of Ashlynne shining so beautifully in such a dark and horrible house.

"Soon. If I have been shown true, soon you will leave these places forever, and then your adventures will really begin! But what have you to do with me? I still haven't seen this, but I will keep watching, Bright Girl. I'll watch and wait because you have been shown to me for a special reason—of that I have no doubt."

"Ma'am?"

"I'm sorry, what?" asked Meredith, removing her sunglasses and looking across the table at the young boy who stood there.

"Would you like more hot water, Ma'am?"

"Yes, please. That would be nice. Thank you." She replied with a nod and a small smile as she replaced her sunglasses against the glare of the late summer sun.

She now looked at days left here in Scotland rather than weeks, and she was both sad to leave and excited to return home. She had not received any updates from Tom on the state of Rosehaven and had, up until recently, chosen to go with the tried and true 'no news is good news' approach. However, as the weeks rolled on she became more concerned and thought returning home was rather a good idea after all.

Chapter 18

om sat in his study and contemplated the email that had come in a few days before. He needed to respond soon, but he couldn't decide how to do so. He missed having Meredith here to bounce these types of things off of, but she was still in Edinburgh. He didn't want to bother her there. Besides, it would be hard to maintain his position of control if he called Meredith every time a decision seemed difficult.

"OK," he said in as firm a voice as he could manage. "We're just going to go for it. If it proves to not be a good fit, then we'll cross that bridge when we come to it. After all, removing a coven member has been done before. How hard could it be?"

He typed out his response to the young woman requesting inner court entrance and hit send.

As he made himself a glass of iced tea in the kitchen, he thought back on his only meeting with Stella Nichols almost six weeks ago. Meredith had just left for Scotland, and Tom had attended a small gathering hosted by another coven about an hour away from his house. He had brought along Camryn for company, and it was she who had introduced them. Stella had been doing outer court work with the hosting coven but, with a planned move further north, had talked to Camryn about joining Dark Grove.

Stella and Cam had hit it off almost immediately, and while Tom didn't dislike her, the dark-haired woman had a brashness to her that could be a little off-putting. That being said, Stella proved to be talented, skilled, and confident. Tom felt that, ultimately, she would be a beneficial addition to the group.

"I hope Meredith agrees," he said to himself as he walked out to the expansive deck that looked out over the fields and the small copse of cedars in the distance. The grove marked a natural spring that bubbled gently up from the loamy earth—a favorite spot for rituals for healing and cleansing.

The afternoon passed pleasantly enough but was cut short by a response from Stella. He agreed to meet her at his favorite bar in Petoskey at around eight o'clock, a town just fifteen miles down the county road.

Tom—showered, shaved, and dressed in his favorite black t-shirt and jeans—entered the restaurant and skirted the hostess with a wave as he chose a seat at the bar to wait for Stella's arrival. The large picture of Ernest Hemingway looked down on the patrons with just a smidgen of disapproval for the flip-flop and t-shirt crowd that now inhabited the watering hole that he used to frequent.

The bartender sat Tom's beer on a napkin and opened a tab, and Tom nodded and smiled. He liked being treated as a regular.

With a slight salute of his drink to the portrait of the famed author, Tom drank the dark ale of which he was most fond and waited for Stella. She wasn't late yet, but she was approaching that line—not a very good first impression to make on the group's leader who you had solicited for membership.

"Hello, you must be Tom Mitchell?"

The slightly musical voice broke into his thoughts, and Tom turned to see the woman he had first met several weeks ago standing to his left.

Pulling out the barstool for Stella to sit, Tom smiled expansively and boomed over the noise of the other patrons.

"Hello! I'm so glad to see you again!" He waved down the bartender to come and take her order.

The evening passed more pleasantly than Tom had expected and glass after glass of the dark ale was consumed. Stella drank the same beer that he did, something that Tom found to be an excellent omen. The conversation turned to the mechanics of magic, covens, and ethics. It was a discussion that always interested Tom, and he approached it as one would a tennis match. Each idea or thought was volleyed or spiked back at the other conversant, more an opponent than a partner to him.

In Stella, he had met his match. For every theory and idea sent her way, she easily batted it back, and with such a unique spin to it that he often missed his chance to respond. So off balance was he by someone who not only would stand up to him, but counter his premises with valid and entertaining theories of her own.

"Yes, but what about balance?" Tom asked, playing devil's advocate as he sipped at what he promised himself would be his last glass of ale.

"What of it?" countered Stella with a grin.

"Power that's not tempered with balance can be dangerous, don't you think so?"

"Not at all. Power is power is power. There is no danger to it, it simply is what it is—a means to an end," asserted the dark-haired young woman sitting next to him.

Tom was thrilled and enlivened with their hours-long tit-for-tat and laughed his deep, boisterous laugh that bounced around the almost-empty bar.

"No danger to power? Tell that to anyone who's had to live under a dictator!"

"But, don't you see? It's not the power that is at fault, but rather who wields it," said

Stella, easily lobbing the ball back into Tom's court.

"Yes, but a dictator without power is just a man yelling into a vacant room."

"Maybe so, maybe not," replied Stella with a sly grin. "I think we've missed the most important aspect of power. Not whether it's good or bad, or should be tempered with balance, but who decides who has power and who doesn't."

The bartender called for the last drinks. Tom settled the tab and headed out into the predawn darkness of downtown Petoskey.

"Thank you, Tom. I've had such a wonderful evening."

"I have, too. I can't remember the last time I closed down a bar!" He laughed as he held her car door open for her. It was an inexpensive two-door sedan that had seen better days, and the door offered up a tinny clang as he shut it after she had settled into the driver's seat.

Stella rolled her window down in response to Tom's knock on the glass and smiled widely at his invitation.

"I know it's not as exciting as a bar," he half-joked, "but if you'd like to come with me to Charlevoix on Tuesday, you can see where your new High Priestess lives. I need to do a house check while she's out of town."

"I would love that. Thank you!" exclaimed Stella, not missing the obvious mention of her High Priestess. She was a member of the coven now! "Will you email me the directions, please?"

Casting a dubious look at her car, Tom asked, "How about I pick you up? Send me your address." He waved as he made his way back to where he had parked.

"That would be great. Thank you!" Stella's bright smile hid the seething anger and embarrassment at Tom's unspoken critique of her car. She knew it was a wreck, and rattled like a coffee can full of marbles when it first started, but it was all she could afford. Stella longed for more; a nice car, a house of her own, and beautiful clothes. However, she grew up flat broke and poor and, for now, had no idea how to change that. Her dreams had led her here, though, to this tiny section of Northwestern Lower Michigan with its massive summer 'cottages,' yachts, and exclusive country clubs. She felt confident that this would be where her life turned around. And Tom and his coven would be instrumental in that—of that, she was certain.

Chapter 19

tella hopped down from the passenger side of Tom's yellow Jeep Wrangler and stared in wonder at the huge white house that towered over them.

"Wow," she whispered to Tom, "is this just one person's house?"

"It belonged to her family, but it's just hers now," replied Tom as he dug the key from his pocket and walked to the service door to the left of the formal entry.

"Aren't we going in the front door?" asked Stella, hurrying to keep up with Tom's long-legged stride.

"Yes, this front door," he laughed. "Rosehaven has multiples of almost everything—including front doors."

"Rosehaven? The house has a name?"

"Yep, it sure does. I think Meredith's mother named it for the rose gardens in the back," explained Tom, opening the door and ushering Stella into the small landing.

Tom slipped past Stella and led the way up the steps, around the hall tree, and into the dining room. Leading the way, he wasn't privy to the unabashed looks of awe and envy that played out on Stella's face as she took in the chandeliers, sculpted wool rugs, imposing European antique furniture, and floor-to-ceiling French doors dressed in old lace.

As she followed Tom through the dining room and into the butler's pantry, Stella couldn't help but let a whisper of wonderment escape her at the built-in, glass-fronted cabinets that held vintage amber glass, Irish crystal goblets, cut glass serving bowls, bone dishes, and serving platters in every size, shape, and material that one could imagine.

"What does she use all of this for?" she called to Tom, who had disappeared into the kitchen.

"Meredith? I don't think she does. Her parents had lots of parties, though."

Stella entered the kitchen and stood aghast all over again.

"Wow. This looks like something out of a movie!" Stella turned in a slow circle taking in the cabinets running up to the high ceilings, the sunroom with its massive potted Ficus tree, overstuffed down settees, and the tumbled marble floor pavers that glowed warmly in the afternoon sun streaming in through the glass panes of the French doors which served as the exterior walls of the space.

"Have you ever seen a kitchen table this long?" laughed Tom as he made his way around the space, checking latches on windows and faucets for drips.

"Never mind the kitchen table. I've never seen anything at all like this!" exclaimed Stella. "I don't think I've ever stayed in a hotel this nice."

"Yeah, and this is just three rooms on the main floor," said Tom as he steered Stella out of the kitchen and back through the butler's pantry. "Wait till you see the main living room, music room, and the library."

"*Main* living room?" asked Stella as she followed Tom into the formal foyer with its grand staircase.

"Like I said, this house has multiples of almost everything."

Stella stood gaping at the enormous double front doors with their leaded glass and old brass fixtures.

Behind her, the music room showcased an antique baby grand piano, two box lyres from England dating back to medieval times, framed sheet music that had yellowed with age, and a tall pedestal holding an ornate crystal vase that mimicked the enormous crystal chandelier gracing the foyer, suspended from the soaring second-floor ceiling.

As the sunlight played off the leaded glass of the doors, bounced off the crystals of the chandelier, and shattered into a million rainbows at the large vase, Stella stood transfixed.

"If this were my house, I would always enter from these doors," she called to Tom, who had moved into the living room to check its French door latches and transom windows.

"What's that?"

"Nothing! Just admiring everything!" she called back as she entered the richly appointed library with its oxblood red walls. The built-in bookcases held leather volumes of classics and modern works, as well as ledgers that looked as if they were part of the bookkeeping of the family. Carved alabaster busts of unknown men took up shelf space here and there, along with framed family pictures and community award statuettes. The hand-painted map of Lake Michigan that adorned the entire ceiling completed the look of old Europe within the New World. Stella was both amazed and incredibly jealous.

As she followed Tom throughout Rosehaven, room to room and floor to floor, her admiration for the easy grandeur of the house grew, as did her resentment of the woman who lived there. It wasn't fair.

"I can't wait for you to meet Meredith," said Tom as he escorted her outside and locked the door behind them.

"Yeah, that will be nice," replied Stella with as much charm as she could muster. She had already decided that she did not like Meredith one bit. Why should one person have so much while she, no matter how hard she worked, remain just this side of destitution?

"I'm sure you'll like her. She helps to run the coven with a pleasant but firm hand," said Tom, starting up the Jeep.

"Yeah, about that," said Stella, raising her voice over the din of the Wrangler's engine.

"How did she come to be in charge of Dark Grove?"

"Let's talk over coffee," Tom suggested, and Stella nodded as the Jeep bumped over the driveway's uneven cobbles and turned right down Michigan Avenue toward the bridge and downtown Charlevoix.

Eliza watched from the second-floor landing windows as Tom and Stella walked down the drive and got into the car that had brought them to Rosehaven. She had stayed quiet and dim during their visit, unsure about how much the dark-haired woman could see or feel. She knew that the large man named Tom, for all of his brashness and knowledge, couldn't see beyond the veil of his own reality.

Though, occasionally, he could sense the change of energy in his environment. But the small woman with the corkscrews of dark curls, she was another thing entirely. Eliza had felt her arrival before the Jeep had turned into the driveway. Waves of deep red and densely black energy had flowed into the home like a river of angry envy. The malice that this one felt for anyone who had something that she coveted was overpowering, and Eliza had made up her mind to not allow her to stay long inside the house.

Forcing her to leave had been fruitless, however. Whether by training or natural ability, the dark-haired Witch came complete with a protective shield of energy so dense that no matter what Eliza sent Stella's way, it simply absorbed into the darkness surrounding her and dissipated into ribbons of nothingness.

After three such attempts, Eliza thought it best to stay clear of this unknown person. If Stella was so strong as to not be affected by anything that was thrown in her direction, it stood to reason that anything that she sent outward could be damaging, to say the least. Eliza stayed dim and out of the way of the two members of Dark Grove coven that traipsed through Rosehaven, one checking the security of the house and the other dreaming of the day that it would be hers.

Tom and Stella settled into the farthest booth from the door at a local hole-in-the-wall diner that had, so far, remained off the radar of the never-ending stream of tourists, referred to as 'fudgies', that were still in abundance- though the summer season was coming to an end.

The waitress greeted them both with a quick smile, sat down a carafe of coffee, dropped a handful of single-serve creamers between them, and took off at a fast clip to the other tables waiting for service.

Stella poured coffee for them both and pushed the pile of creamers out of the way.

"This is nice," she said, looking around at the plain-Jane dining room.

"Well, I don't know about 'nice,' but it's a great place to have a decent cup of coffee and not have to trip over tourists," said Tom.

"Don't they want the tourists' dollars, though?" asked Stella, taking a sip of her coffee.

"I don't think it matters to them. They've been here for decades and are open year-round, unlike so many of the other places that put all of their eggs into the summer-money basket. Here, you can get a great breakfast or lunch and never-ending coffee in January or June."

"I see," mused Stella, not understanding at all. The whole tourist town thing was completely new to her, but the amount of money involved intrigued her a great deal.

"So, tell me, how did you meet Meredith?" she asked, trying to bring the conversation back to the coven.

Tom talked about his first call to those of like mind after he had finished his training and the gathering of the respondents at his home. He regaled her with stories of the different personalities, their quirks, and their talents. They laughed at his descriptions of the motley group that had become Dark Grove Coven.

"You're traditionally trained, yes?" asked Stella, pouring more coffee for them both.

"Yes. I have my third-degree cords and have been ordained to start a coven of my own."

"That's wonderful. How long does that take to achieve? Earning the three cords, I mean?"

"Well, it can depend," Tom said, sitting back in his seat and crossing his arms one over the other.

Stella recognized his 'I am about to impart important knowledge to you' body language and tried hard to not roll her eyes. She had a feeling that she would need Tom Mitchell squarely on her side, and that meant playing to his ego. Besides, he might have information that could be valuable to her.

"When you start traditional training in Wicca, you begin as a Dedicant, which means you are accepted into the group on a trial basis for one year and one day. During that time, either the Dedicant or the High Priest or Priestess can choose to not continue the relationship. The Dedicant is released with love and trust. If, after a year and a day, everyone decides that it is a good fit, then the Dedicant is brought in as a full member with an oath-taking ceremony. This is when the first-degree cords are given and study is begun. From that point on, the first-degree Witch is a full member of the coven, participating in all rituals and completing a course of lessons about the Craft. Within a year— or up to eighteen months—when the High Priest and Priestess deem them ready, the Witch is brought into a ritual circle and asked to perform certain tasks and chants from memory. If they succeed, they are conferred with the next set of cords that mark them as a second-degree Witch. The next step on the journey can take anywhere from one to three years and can be very difficult. The second degree requires the Witch to go inward and downward, traversing their own psyche. It is the Dark Night of the Soul or Persephone's Descent. It can be perilous, but ultimately freeing, for those who choose to make the trip."

Tom took a sip of his coffee and waved to the waitress. She approached and took Tom's order of a sandwich and more coffee for Stella.

"You're not hungry?" he asked, pushing his coffee cup out of his way and taking a drink of his ice water.

"No, I ate earlier," Stella lied. She didn't have enough money to eat, but the coffee killed her appetite, so she kept her cup full.

"After the second degree, the Witch gets her last set of cords?" asked Stella, prompting Tom to finish his story.

"Yes, and no. During the second degree, the Witch can also work on areas of specialty and be awarded cords for those. For example, when a course of study for herbs and tinctures is successfully completed, a green cord is conferred. If the study of Sabbats and celebrations is completed, a gold cord is added. If you attend a gathering with us, you will see elders with up to eleven or twelve cords around their waists, though some do choose to stop with the third-degree cord which is silver, and the animal pelt mantle that signifies a High Priest or Priestess of a coven."

Stella blinked rapidly, trying to process all the information that Tom had just provided.

"I have a question, or maybe two," she laughed.

"Shoot," said Tom, taking a bite of the sandwich that the waitress had deposited in front of him during his monologue.

"What is a gathering?"

"A yearly gathering of all of the covens within the Dark Tree Clan."

"So, there's more than one coven?" asked Stella, trying to not stare at the pile of french fries on Tom's plate.

"Oh, yeah. There are about thirty now."

"What coven did you belong to before starting Dark Grove?"

"I trained in the Blackstone Hearth Coven with our founder, Midnight Bluestone," replied Tom, sounding boastful.

Understanding that this was seen as something very prestigious, Stella practically gushed, "Oh! I have some of her books! Do you actually know her? That's amazing!"

Tom took a big bite of his sandwich, chewed, and then smiled at Stella.

"Yeah, it's pretty cool. She's an incredible teacher."

"And Meredith, did she train with Midnight Bluestone, too?"

"Oh, no. Meredith wasn't part of any of this until I formed Dark Grove Coven."

"Wait, all of that training that you just talked about, Meredith hasn't completed it? How is she a High Priestess?"

"I'm training Meredith as we go along. She is currently a second-degree Witch. You'll see that she has both a red cord and a black cord. When she returns from Europe, she will be tested and will receive her third-degree cords as soon as I can gather enough elders from the Dark Tree Clan to attend the ritual."

The creeping tone of defensiveness in Tom's voice wasn't lost on Stella, and she back-tracked quickly, though not before making a note to herself that perhaps Tom Mitchell had not followed the rules for elevations quite as he should have. Stella might need this information in the future.

"Oh, yes. Of course! I mean, who better to train his High Priestess than the High Priest himself?" smiled Stella, helping herself to a single fry from Tom's plate.

Tom smiled and pushed the plate into the center of the table, indicating that she should help herself to the contents.

Stella nodded her thanks, took another fry, and smiled at her host.

"When can we talk about my dedicating to Dark Grove Coven, Tom?"

Chapter 20

Meredith replayed the argument she and Tom had over the addition of Stella to the coven for at least the thousandth time, simultaneously sick of thinking about it and obsessively picking apart the row that they had had so many weeks ago.

"What do you mean she's been accepted as a Dedicant?"

Meredith eyed Tom over her bottle of beer as he stared out over the railing of the deck toward the healing spring behind his house.

"I mean exactly what I just said, Meredith. Stella has dedicated to Dark Grove Coven," he replied, not meeting her gaze.

Meredith seethed at the casualness with which Tom set aside her position to do as he pleased.

She took a long drink of her beer and looked out at where Tom stared, the healing springs. The way she felt at this news, the water there would bubble up in a roiling eruption should she even dip a toe into its beautiful pools.

"I think I should have been consulted on this," she tried again, keeping her voice level.

"You were out of the country, and I had it handled," he replied, matching her tone.

"You encouraged me to take that trip, Tom!"

"Yes, I did. I thought it would do you some good to get out and see what other aspects of the Craft were out there, but you can't think that the entire coven would simply be placed on hold with your absence, Meredith." His tone was carefully modulated, as if he were speaking to a dimwitted child. Or a hysterical woman.

"This is why a coven should have both a High Priest and a Priestess. The life of the coven moves on, and if one is not available to perform their duties, then the other will be."

Meredith studied the horizon, watching the dark clouds there match her mood. Tom made perfect sense, and she knew that was exactly what he was going for, but she didn't miss some key points in his justifications.

First of all, there was the unspoken accusation that she had left and was somehow derelict in her duties, as if she has run off as an AWOL Witch without a care in the world. The other thing that she caught was the omission of the word 'high' in front of her title of Priestess. No matter the appearance of a perfectly sensible discussion on the matter, Meredith had the distinct feeling that Tom was attempting to spin this scenario as something that she had dropped the ball on, and she didn't appreciate it one bit.

"What was the hurry in dedicating her, anyway? In the past, we have conducted dedications and cord rites in February at Imbolc. Why did Stella need to be dedicated during Midsummer?"

"It was a time that worked well for everyone, Meredith! Why are you making such a big deal about this? Everyone likes Stella—you included! I'm not understanding your objections."

Noting the non-answer and choosing to let it lay for now, Meredith finished her beer, stood, and went into Tom's kitchen where she rinsed the bottle and placed it into the recycling bin.

"I'm going home now. I don't enjoy fighting, and I don't see us resolving this," she called through the sliding door to where he sat, staring out at the backyard.

"At least not today," she said to herself as she exited the small house at the front door and made her way to her car.

Lost in her memories of the argument, Meredith barely registered that she had come in from the back porch to refill her coffee cup. Sipping the rich brew, so much more to her liking than the never-ending tea in Scotland, she ruminated over the events that took place when she first arrived home. What continued to nag at her was how she had so easily been looped out of her own group. How did that happen? More importantly, why did it happen? And as for Tom's assertion that she liked Stella, that wasn't true at all.

"Social niceties do not a friendship make," she said as she returned to the wicker swing on the expansive back porch. It was September now. The gardens, just barely awake and beginning to green when she left for Edinburgh, were now the deep, mellow colors of late summer—golden yellows, deep mauves, blood reds, and darkest greens. Only the banks of Rosa Rugosa plants continued to produce the delicate pinks of early summer. Soon there would be more red rose hips than pink blossoms, something that always signaled the end of the summer for Meredith, more so than even maple leaves tinged orange.

Despite the peaceful drowsiness of her gardens, Meredith continued to fret over the situation with Stella, Tom, and the coven. It bothered her that she did not care for Stella, only because she couldn't put her finger on why. Stella was appropriately deferential to her when she arrived back from Europe— polite, helpful, and good-natured. But there was something there, just under the surface, that set Meredith's teeth on edge. She felt she had met her before, but couldn't recall where or when. To make it even more maddening, she seemed to be the only one who felt like this. The rest of the coven—Riley included—saw only a cheerful, interested new member who participated happily in whatever chore or job she was given. Tom, especially, seemed enamored by Stella, as did Camryn.

"Am I jealous?" Meredith asked herself for the umpteenth time. Still, in her heart of hearts, she knew the answer to be no.

"I'm hurt. I'm confused, but I'm not jealous," she declared, needing to hear her convictions aloud.

"There's something not right, an undercurrent I'm feeling that wasn't there when I left. I don't know what is going on, but if Tom thinks he can gaslight me into thinking that this rush job with Stella is my fault, he's wrong. Very wrong."

Meredith watched as the fuzzy bumble bees bumped and buzzed around the roses, seemingly drunk on the fragrance and nectar of the late summer blooms. She dearly wished that her convictions spoken aloud would magically put to rest the looping scenes that played out in her mind. But she knew they wouldn't. They hadn't yet, and it had been over a month since her return.

"The show must go on," she said with a rueful chuckle as she went into the house to change and get ready for the ritual of Mabon. Meredith had extended the invitation to have the ritual at Rosehaven in her gardens, but Tom had decided against it. Tradition had them conducting rituals in the field behind his house, and that's where they would stay. Meredith tried to see this as just a quirk of Tom's, but a persistent feeling of foreboding covered her coven activities now. She had considered participating less and letting them do as they saw fit, but her ego—as well as her very real sense of duty to her coven mates— stopped her from doing that.

As she folded her black ceremonial robes and added the twist of her cords on top, Meredith steeled herself for the afternoon to come. No matter the strange undercurrent of off-kilter energy, she knew she was still the High Priestess of the coven, and she would conduct herself as such.

Placing her ritual wear into a canvas tote, she sat on her bed for a minute and collected herself.

"I need you," she whispered and waited for her owl to stir within her breast. Feeling the raptor settle heavily within her, she felt secure.

"I don't like feeling like I'm entering the proverbial lion's den," she said as she descended the back staircase, "but having you close makes me feel much better. Thank you, my friend."

As she piloted her small car out onto the street and toward Tom's house just outside Horton Bay, it occurred to her that this would be the second Mabon celebrated at what could now only be called the Dark Grove

Covenstead. She couldn't shake the feeling that disaster awaited.

Chapter 21

The coven sat, stood, and lounged as each saw fit around Tom's living room, their plates filled with the assorted treats both sweet and savory that made up the Sabbat potluck, which had become the traditional end of their celebrations. The conversation flowed easily, and even Stella seemed to be more at peace, being a part of a group rather than trying to maintain her imagined position of uniqueness. Meredith very much appreciated it. And though it still bothered her a great deal that she couldn't pinpoint her dislike or feeling of familiarity for the other woman, Meredith was happy to enjoy this small measure of camaraderie. She had dearly missed it these past months.

Taking a sip of her wine, Meredith watched as Rose and Nathan cuddled on the couch and smiled. She enjoyed the realness of their relationship.

"Everybody! Gather 'round. I have something to show you all!" Tom's voice boomed out from the dining room, startling Meredith out of her daydreams of wedded bliss.

The coven members fanned out around the dining room table where Tom, having relegated the remnants of the potluck to the kitchen counters, waited. In front of him was a plain wooden box, obviously quite old.

"What's up?" asked Micheal as he moved towards the box, arm outstretched.

"No! Don't touch it!" Tom barked, sounding angrier than he intended.

Micheal snatched his arm back in alarm, his face registering his surprise at the rebuke.

"Tom, what the hell?" snapped Meredith, watching Micheal blush and step behind Rose.

"Sorry, Micheal. I didn't mean to sound angry," said Tom with a forced grin. "I have a group activity for us to try, and it requires that we *not* touch the box," he explained, trying to soften his tone.

Meredith, catching the strained tone in Tom's voice, watched quietly as he cleared his throat and smiled again at the group that he had called into the room.

"I want us all to try something together," he began. "This box contains something, and I want us, as a group, to find out what that is. Without physically touching it."

"Why aren't you doing this for us, Meredith?" asked Riley.

Tom glared at the interruption, and Meredith raised an eyebrow in his direction.

"Yes, Tom. Why have I not been asked to see what the box contains?"

Tom kept his tone friendly and light, not wanting to begin yet another point of contention between Meredith and himself.

"You are already quite adept at seership. I thought this might be a good way to gather our collective strength and let those who are not as practiced in the art gain some experience."

The coven murmured in agreement, and Meredith added nothing more. Tom had made it quite clear that this was his show. The buzzing of the coven and Meredith's feeling of unease conjured images of an angry beehive in her mind.

"So much for the warmth and fuzziness of the post-ritual gathering," she mumbled.

"I'm sorry," whispered Riley, recognizing the interaction between Tom and Meredith as one more slight directed by her High Priest at her High Priestess.

Meredith smiled wanly at her friend, then forced herself to direct her attention to the production in front of her. Lately, Tom exhausted her with his never-ending *bigness*. He filled whatever space he was in, demanding attention and displacing all energy not his own. When she wasn't out of sorts, she found this intriguing. The man didn't take other people's energy; he simply eclipsed everything that was not his own. Trying to maintain her own agency in the face of that depleted her just as much as if he were actually siphoning energy directly from her.

"This box was my father's, and now it is mine. He brought it home from New Orleans many years ago. As far as I know, it has never been opened. There is no key."

"Couldn't you just pry it open?" asked Rose.

"I would prefer to not damage it. It's very old," replied Tom with a smile in her direction. Rose rarely spoke, but when she did, she was direct and to the point.

"Plus," Tom continued, "since the contents are a mystery, I thought this might offer us all the chance to delve into territory that has, up until now, been the domain of our Priestess!"

Tom grinned condescendingly at Meredith before sweeping the rest with a more paternal smile. The slight differences in expressions weren't lost on Meredith.

Stella watched the interactions between Tom, Meredith, and Riley with great interest. There seemed to be a definite fracture between the coven's High Priest and his Priestess, and this provided the potential for her to become more than just another member if it continued.

"So! Let's all give this a try, shall we?" boomed Tom, speaking as if he stood on a stage in front of a crowd of thousands rather than in his dining room surrounded by a group of less than a dozen.

"I want everyone to drop their arms to their sides and roll one shoulder at a time up and back, then gently shake your arms. Once you have done that, please close your eyes."

Tom watched as the coven did as he asked. When each member had closed their eyes, he continued.

"Now, take a deep breath in through your nose. Hold it for a count of three. Good. Now, release it gently through your mouth."

As they went through the mechanics of grounding and centering, Meredith forced herself to follow along as a part of the group rather than one in charge of it. It was a strange position for her to be in.

"Very good," crooned Tom in a soothing voice. "Now, I want each of you to envision the box in as much detail as possible—the lid, hinges, the color of the wood, all of it."

Tom waited as the coven members stood before him, eyes closed, and breathing deeply in a deep meditative state.

"Good. Now that you have a clear picture of the box in your mind, I want you to try to touch it. Reach out and feel the wood. Is it rough? Smooth? Are there bumps or divots?"

Tom continued the exercise, bringing the coven through a meditation that covered all of their senses in the spiritual or astral realm.

"Nicely done. You have all seen, touched, smelled, and listened to the box as it sits within your mind. Now comes the last part of our exercise," said Tom, his voice pitched low and almost monotonous to not scatter the energies of the almost-hypnotic state that he had brought his coven to.

"It is time for you to open the box. Whether that is with a key of your own conjuring or by simply lifting the lid is an individual decision, but at my count of five, each of you will open the box that you have crafted within your mind. Ready? Now, one...two...three...four...," Tom paused just a bit and then, "Five. Open your box."

Tom Mitchell watched as each coven member's face registered the effects of their activity. Rose seemed her usual undeterred self. Nathan's face had arranged itself into a quizzical visage. Micheal's cheeks were drawn and pale, and his forehead furrowed in concentration. The sisters, Riley and Camryn, stood motionless, their shoulders almost touching, wearing an identical expression of disbelief. Disbelief in the activity or in what each could see, Tom didn't know. Stella wore a smile of delight, and Tom found himself hoping beyond hope that she had succeeded in opening the box. When he turned to look at Meredith, he saw that she had dropped, lifeless, into the nearest chair, her eyes moving rapidly behind her closed lids and her lips pressed together in fear. The only sound in the room was the soft mews of fright coming from the comatose form of his Priestess.

Despite the distressing position of Meredith, Tom forced himself to slowly count to ten before clapping his hands together three times in rapid succession, bringing the coven back to this time and space. He watched as, as a group, they opened their eyes, blinking as if just waking from a long nap, and looked around the room. All of them, that is, except Meredith, who lay across the chair she had dropped into, her eyes moving rapidly behind her lids and her body twitching violently every few seconds.

"Oh, my god! Meredith!" cried Riley as she dropped to her knees in front of Meredith. The others began to voice their concern as Tom stood there, mute and afraid.

Stella made a calculated decision and chose to move to Tom, standing at his side as the others crowded around Meredith.

Raising her voice over the buzzing of her coven mates, Stella took charge.

"Hey, everyone, back up and give her some room! She's just gone deeper than any of us did and needs a few more minutes to come back. Riley, will you please get the lemonade pitcher from the kitchen? Micheal, could you bring in the last of the cookies? We need to get some sugar and carbs in us before we discuss what we all saw."

They all looked up to see Stella smiling gently and standing next to Tom, whose face was in the process of trying to rearrange itself from confusion and concern to serenity and control.

Riley did as she was told, not because she was comfortable with Stella telling her to, but because she needed something practical to do. She had seen Meredith go deeply into trances before, so she chose to believe Stella's assessment of the situation. Micheal followed Riley, thinking that if she thought it was OK, then it must be.

The magic of Midsummer is both a boon and a curse. Stella knew this and took advantage of the bright sunlit energies to both illuminate and blind, showcasing herself as one who is capable of leading while, at the same time, hiding her discovery of what lay within the box.

Chapter 22

eredith tumbled over and over in a black void, no sound, no breeze, no smell—nothing at all.

How could the box contain nothing at all?

She had followed along with Tom's guided hypnosis, making sure to not jump ahead of the instructions, wanting to participate as part of the coven. Although, it was an unfamiliar position for her since she was used to doing this sort of thing on her own.

The box loomed large in front of Meredith, floating in full three-dimensional glory within her mind. She stepped into the blackness and followed Tom's directions to examine it using all of her senses. She added a small table for it to sit on. Other than that, she conducted her perusal exactly as he directed.

There was nothing unusual or unexpected with the feel, scent, sound, or look of the box, and Meredith tried to not feel irritated with the endeavor. After all, it was an exercise, and maybe that was the whole of it—examine the box within a trance state.

And then he began his countdown, which would end with each of them opening the lid.

Meredith concentrated on the box, trying to decide if she needed a key or if it would open of its own accord. Off in the distance, she could hear the High Priest droning on toward the final number of his sequence, but most of her attention was on the box that sat in front of her—a perfect replica of the one that he had set before them on his dining room table.

She decided to simply lift the lid rather than attempt to conjure a key. As Tom spoke the last of his countdown, she reached out and lifted the lid, its wood smooth and silky beneath her fingers.

And in she fell, tumbling head over heels through a black nothingness the likes of which she had never encountered. Her fall seemed to last at once forever and for just a second or two before she landed with a thump at the base of a large tree. The air was a swirling lavender mist and smelled both sweet and spicy, like an herb garden ready for harvest.

"Hello?" whispered Meredith, standing on shaky legs.

There was no reply and very little sound except for a faint humming that seemed to be the song of this place and not a response to her call.

She noticed that the box didn't make the journey with her and wondered where she had gone wrong with Tom's exercise. It had seemed so straightforward, yet here she was in an unknown place without the box.

"Or is *this* what was in the box?" Shaking her head, she dismissed the idea. The box wasn't a portal—she would have seen that from the get-go.

"I need you!" Meredith said in a clear voice, fighting the need to whisper in this strange land. She waited and watched, but there was no sign of her owl.

The first tendrils of fear snaked their way into her chest as Meredith stepped away from the trunk of the tree and wandered down the packed dirt lane that stretched out before her, disappearing at the horizon.

"I'm not sure if I'm meant to be Dorothy or Alice, but I'm not happy with this at all," groused the Witch as she stepped carefully over stones and sticks that lay here and there along the way. While she didn't know where she was, she had enough experience in other-realm travels to know that not every rock was indeed a rock, and she had no intentions of angering some astral-nasty laying in wait for her disguised as a pebble.

"I'm not sure who Alice or Dorothy is, Dear, but if you're Meredith Cadwell, then this beautiful creature belongs with you."

The raspy voice and the smell of cigarette smoke startled Meredith so completely that she barely held in a squawk of alarm as she jumped and turned in a very poor model of a pirouette. All in all, the normally regal woman resembled an awkward middle schooler who had just been caught skipping class.

"Who the hell are you?" spat Meredith between gritted teeth. She was well aware of her less-than-graceful turn and resented having been taken by surprise.

Mimi regarded the discombobulated blonde with interest. Her hair was disheveled and fell in her face, partially obscuring her eyes, though the irritation couldn't hide behind the blonde wisps. Not by a long shot.

"I'm Miriam, Dear. Thank you for coming."

Meredith gaped at the woman who sat in an incongruous chintz armchair and dressed in a cartoonish Andrew Sisters-inspired get-up, complete with victory-rolled hair and a severe wool suit with shoulder pads. The woman crossed one stockinged leg over the other and blew three perfect smoke rings, all the while smiling serenely at her.

"But where did you come from?" asked Meredith, her head swiveling back and forth. She had already walked past the spot where the woman now sat in her armchair. As odd as this place was, Meredith felt certain that she wouldn't have missed her.

"Well, Dear, that is a question with many answers, but for now I am just here," said Mimi, spreading her arms wide. The owl on her shoulder mimicked her gesture by spreading its enormous wings as it balanced itself on the back of Mimi's chair.

"That's my owl," stated Meredith, her eyes squinting in disapproval.

"Ah, there she is," laughed Mimi. "The strong Witch I was told I would meet here."

"Come to me," demanded Meredith, and the owl lifted itself from the back of the chair, flew a lazy circle above the treetops, then came to rest on Meredith's shoulder—the silver cord running from Meredith to the bird clearly visible.

Confident that she had taken the upper hand, Meredith regarded Mimi, who sat inhaling and blowing smoke rings.

"That's bad for you, you know."

"So I've been told," laughed Mimi.

"Are you dead, then?" asked Meredith.

"Well, that, too, is a question with several answers. For now, let's just say that we are both getting to know each other in a safe place."

"And why do we need to know each other?" asked Meredith, her tone icy.

"You and I have a task to complete, Meredith. It's been a long time in the making, but the two of us will make sure that the ending is as it should be."

"I need a bit more information than that," replied Meredith, not warming up to the meeting at all.

"Most of that will be provided as the story unfolds, Dear. For now, you should see this."

Mimi blew a curtain of smoke out in front of them. As it drifted away into the trees, Meredith saw an ornate mirror hanging in the lavender air.

"That's clever, Miriam."

"Oh, call me Mimi, Dear. All my friends do!"

"Are we friends, then, Mimi?"

"Well, I sincerely hope we can be because we have quite the job ahead of us, and it would make the work so much less awful," said Mimi with a sad smile.

"I'm not liking the sound of this at all."

"I imagine not, Dear, but it's something that must be done, and done right this time. Please, look in the mirror."

Meredith turned to look directly into the mirror that the woman in the flowered chair had so casually conjured.

The glass grew gray and misty. It swirled as if Mimi's smoke was trapped within. Slowly, a bright spot in the center of the swirling grayness grew larger until Meredith could make out a scene within the confines of the mirror's frame.

"Is that—?"

"Yes, Dear. That's her. She shines so brightly, doesn't she?" said Mimi with a sad smile.

"Do you know who she is?"

"Yes, I know her well."

"My owl has shown me this child before. What does she have to do with me?"

"She will set you free."

Meredith snorted rudely. "Great, I've been waylaid by a traveling preacher. I'm not interested in your religion."

"I'm not the preacher. He'll come along later," said Mimi, smiling at the confusion on the imperious woman's face. "Let's not be difficult. We have a lot to do, you and I."

"But you're talking in riddles!"

"Oh, but I'm not," said Mimi. "This child will absolutely set you free, but that won't happen for a little while yet. Ashlynne has some things that she must accomplish before she comes to your rescue."

"Her name is Ashlynne?" Meredith's voice was small. She had wondered who this girl was for so long, and now she finally had a name.

"Yes, Dear. Ashlynne Barrow."

"She shines."

"Indeed, she does," smiled Mimi.

Meredith stared at the scenes that played out in the depths of Mimi's mirror, feeling at once sad for the girl and excited that she may finally know why she had been shown the child.

"How will a child set me free?" she asked over her shoulder, keeping her eyes on the mirror.

"She won't be a child when that happens. She will be older and tried mightily before she's asked to tackle your problem."

"Who will ask her, and what problem?" asked Meredith, still very confused.

"Why, you will, Dear."

Meredith gaped at the woman who smiled back so benignly.
"But—"

"Patience, Meredith. First, some things must be done. When you return, you will need to teach the coven about the powers of the Journey Stone."

"How do you know about the Journey Stone?"

Ignoring her, Mimi continued, "Then you will keep careful note of what the owl shows you. Write it all down if you must. When the time comes, you will send the letter that will begin the ending of all of this. Do you understand?"

"Not at all!" snapped Meredith.

"Teach them the power of the Journey Stone and mind what the owl tells you. Those are the two most important things for now. When it's time, we'll discuss the monk."

"Wait, there's a monk?" squeaked Meredith. "I thought you were kidding about a preacher!"

"There is a monk, Dear. When he comes to you, you must let him in. All of this must be accomplished in order to end what was started so long ago."

"But you haven't *told* me anything!"

"Just teach them to use the Journey Stone, Meredith. Everything else will follow."

Meredith came to. Riley sat by her side, casting concerned glances around the now-empty dining room.

"Where is everyone?"

"Oh! You're awake! Thank goodness! I was getting really worried," smiled Riley, gently noting the smudges of dark circles under her friend's eyes. "Are you OK?"

"Yeah, I think so," said Meredith, sitting up slowly.

"Want some lemonade or a cookie?"

"No, thank you. What I want to know is where the coven is," said Meredith wearily, noting the empty dining room.

"They're all in the living room with Stella and Tom, discussing what they saw in the box during the guided meditation."

"Are they now?" said Meredith in a steely voice as she pulled herself off the chair and straightened her hair.

"Let's you and I go see what that was, shall we?"

Riley's smile faltered at the tone of Meredith's voice and the set of her jaw.

"Of course, Meredith," whispered Riley, trailing behind her as she made her way back into the living room to rejoin the coven.

Chapter 23

Stella, tired of scanning reference books and lesson pages, let her mind wander back to the night when she met the Faerie. Tom had called them all into his dining room the evening of their Mabon Sabbat and led them through a guided meditation exercise which would, he hoped, allow them each to view the inside of the box. It was an ordinary old box, and Stella had at first wondered why Tom didn't just pry the lid open—a question that Rose had asked as well. Tom's answer seemed pretty vague, but watching the undercurrent of the power-play between Tom and Meredith sweetened the deal immensely. Stella was more than happy to participate in any activity that was previously the sole domain of the High Priestess.

Stella sat with her eyes closed and followed Tom's suggestions. As she progressed through the meditation, she felt a pleasant heaviness in her limbs, and her head nodded down, her chin resting on her chest.

The longer the exercise went on, the more Tom's voice receded. Stella could still hear enough to follow his instructions, but her consciousness had become securely anchored within the astral realm in which she had entered.

At the conclusion of the High Priest's countdown, Stella reached out and opened her version of the box. At first, there was nothing she could see except for a layer of dusty soil, some dried herbs, and a few rocks.

"What the hell? Is *this* why we went through all of this rigmarole?" asked Stella, her voice strangely hollow in this non-place.

"All of this for some garden junk stashed in an old box?"

As she grumbled and complained about the lack of anything interesting stashed inside Tom's box, a sly chuckle from the box echoed outward as if the box were leagues deep, rather than only a few inches.

Stella stood still, every part of her now alert. As the disturbing laughter diminished, a slick of green and brown flowed out and into the blackness, floating like a visible illness between Stella and the box.

As she watched, a growing fear gnawed at her. She suddenly felt how alone she was in this black void. Why hadn't Tom instructed them to make a room, a house, or a garden—something other than this nothingness of black?

"Ssssstteeelllaaaaaaaa." Just a whisper, but it ran up and down Stella's spine like a sharp blade.

In her altered state, Stella closed her eyes against whatever was whispering from the box. It did no good, and images flowed into her mind that transfixed and amazed her. Gone was her fear, gone was the annoyance of the exercise. The promises made by the creature inside the box had replaced those with excitement, glee, and a deep motivation to make all of them a reality once she came out of this trance.

"Do you see, Stella? It can all be yours if you let me out," whispered the voice.

"What are you?" asked Stella, never once thinking that the question could result in an answer that would change her world and everyone in it.

"My kind has been called many things. The Good Folk, The Fair Folk, The Gentry, and many more. Our kind doesn't take well to being named by the likes of your kind, Stella. But no matter the name I choose, I can provide you with all that you've wanted."

"Everything you've shown me can be mine?"

"Everything and more."

"I want a house like Rosehaven," whispered Stella.

"No, Stella," said the voice with a gleeful laugh. "You want *Rosehaven*, not a house like it."

Stella smiled wickedly. She had never thought it possible to have the actual house that she coveted.

"Not only is it possible, it will be done. Rosehaven, and anything else that you desire, will be yours," said the voice, easily reading what flowed through Stella's thoughts.

"What do I need to do?"

"You must let me out of this box. We can do wondrous things together, you and I, but you must free me first."

"Tell me how," urged Stella, feeling her hold on this realm becoming more and more tenuous.

"There is a ritual that is already performed by the Dark Grove coven, but certain words have been omitted by Meredith. You must put those words back into the ritual—reignite their magic—and then my freedom will be secured."

"That's all?"

"That is the beginning, Stella."

The memory made her smile all over again; everything that she had ever wanted would be hers, but she needed to free the Faerie before that could happen.

And a Faerie it was because Stella, wanting to know just exactly what she was conversing with, searched the library for references to The Good Folk, The Fair Folk, and other terms that the thing had used with the overwhelming number of results pointing to Faerie or Fae.

This revelation led to more research because Stella had questions. What kind of

Faerie talked to humans? Were Faeries dangerous? Can humans work with Faeries? And last, but very important, can humans control Faeries?

The search for each question's answer brought her books and authors spanning the globe, but it seemed to Stella that the majority of the information came from the British Isles. Stella had to admit that most of these authors warned against partnering with the Fae because they were wily and not to be trusted. They also warned that any interaction came at a higher price for humans than for The Good Folk, but Stella dismissed this; her case was unique. The Faerie needed her to release it. In return, Stella would receive Rosehaven and the wealth that went with it. The contract seemed pretty even to her, despite the warnings to not engage. The only thing that didn't seem accurate for *her* Faerie was that it spoke in a plain conversational manner. The folklorists all claimed that the Fae spoke in rhyme and in such a way as to impart easily misinterpreted information for pacts that they desired to be made. This Fae did not, but Stella set the discrepancy aside, deciding that it had chosen to speak plainly because its freedom was at stake.

"Or maybe it had been in that box for so long that it had learned modern speech patterns?" suggested Camryn, who Stella had enlisted as her strongest ally in the quest to free the Faerie.

It surprised Stella that after only after a short time of incredulous questions, Camryn came on board and helped plan the thing's escape. Of course, being promised a powerful position within the group and all that her heart desired didn't hurt to sweeten the deal.

Now both women spent every free minute they had scouring the published books and unpublished lessons of their clan founder, Midnight Bluestone, for the lost wording in their group's rituals.

"When we find it, do you think it will be obvious why Meredith chose to not use it or teach it to us?" asked Camryn during their most recent deep dive into their combined coven degree lessons.

"Obvious, how?" asked Stella, forming the words carefully around the pencil that she held between her teeth, used to underline a possible phrase, stir her coffee, and chew on as each need presented itself.

"I mean, will it be words or phrases that are dangerous or dark? Maybe it's something that we shouldn't use, and that's why Meredith removed it."

Stella snorted, "More than likely we will find that the omitted words will level the playing field, removing power from Meredith—something she would never allow."

"Yeah, I guess that makes sense."

As the day wore on and the sky turned a brilliant orange outside the windows of

Stella's tiny apartment, both women grew weary with what seemed to be the never-ending search.

"Want me to make us some coffee?" asked Camryn, as familiar now with Stella's kitchen as she was with her own.

"Um, yeah. That would be nice," mumbled Stella, still scanning page after page in the massive three-ring binder that held her study notes and degree lessons for Dark Grove.

Camryn, tired of the chore, sat down with a book from Stella's bookcase while she waited for the coffee to finish brewing.

"Hey, what's this?" she called across the room.

"What?" asked Stella, not bothering to look at Camryn or the object she held.

Walking over to where the other woman sat hunched over her notebook, Camryn thrust the small book under Stella's nose and covered the pages of the notebook that she had been staring at for over an hour.

"This, Stella!" said Camryn, jabbing her finger at the passage halfway down the page that had caught her attention.

"It's just the circle casting, Cam. The one we use all the time. I thought you had that memorized by now."

"I do, which is why I noticed that *this* one is not the same one as in our lessons, or what's used by the coven," snapped Camryn. She was—by now—tired, under-caffeinated, and sick of Stella's attitude.

"Wow, OK. Chill," whispered Stella, just loud enough for Camryn to hear.

She moved the book closer and read the circle casting that Camryn insisted differed from the one they used. Stella thought for sure that the other woman was mistaken. The book was written by Midnight Bluestone but not published for the public; it was a small ritual handbook given to covens within the clan so the formats would remain consistent throughout them all.

Stella skimmed the passage quickly and then stopped, her eyes fixing on a passage that she had never heard nor used within their rituals or celebrations. She looked up at Camryn, a smile wide and triumphant on her face.

"That's it, isn't it?" asked Cam, trying to sound more elated than boastful.

"Oh, my god. Cam! This is it! It has to be! Good job!" laughed Stella, wrapping her co-conspirator in a hug.

Camryn laughed and quickly extricated herself from Stella. She admired her but was never completely comfortable around her, and finding the passage did nothing to change that.

"Coffee, then?" she asked, grabbing mugs from the cupboard over the sink.

"With some whiskey, I think!" laughed Stella. "Irish Coffee seems pretty fitting right now, doesn't it?"

Chapter 24

The Journey Stone sat on the kitchen table. It looked like a gray Easter egg with a swath of shimmering white banding around its middle. It wasn't terribly large, or small, and aside from the white band of quartz was just about the dullest stone Meredith could imagine. There was absolutely nothing about it that suggested the great power it contained, and that was exactly as she would have it. Nothing so devoid of glitz or sparkle was likely to be stolen.

Having finished her lunch and loaded the dirty dishes into the dishwasher, Meredith sighed. It was getting closer for her to leave for Horton Bay. Time to make herself presentable.

She missed the early days of the study group and its resulting coven when everyone was friendly and without hidden agendas. She missed feeling like she belonged and was valued. Most importantly, she missed her friends that had become like family. Over time, something had crept into the group, an undercurrent of distrust. Lately, it seemed as if everyone had an unspoken resentment, and Meredith couldn't quite put her finger on when it began. Was it when she went to Scotland for the summer? The addition of Stella? Or had she changed so much that she, herself, simply didn't fit in any longer?

"You have to admit that you've been keeping a lot of secrets," she said to her image as she applied a bit of makeup before leaving the house.

The owl, meeting Mimi during the guided meditation that Tom facilitated, and the knowledge of Ashlynne were all things that she had kept to herself.

"And don't forget the Journey Stone! How are you going to explain that you've had this knowledge since your trip to Scotland and kept it to yourself all this time?"

She gazed at herself in the mirror. A woman approaching her thirties with frown lines and crow's feet showing more and more each day. Her eyes were direct and, at times, intimidating. Her mouth seemed more naturally held in a straight line than curved upward in a smile. In short, she looked as stressed and saddened as she felt. She also had no answer to her last self-directed question.

"I guess I'll cross that bridge when I get to it," she whispered as she exited her room and descended the stairs.

"At least my Shining Girl is doing alright," Meredith continued her conversation with herself as she located her notebook, a light sweater, a pair of loafers, and some mints. She wrapped the Journey Stone in a swatch of black satin and deposited it into a deep purple velvet bag. She placed it carefully inside the side pocket of the larger tote to bring along to an afternoon at Tom's with the coven.

Meredith had sent the owl on a semi-regular basis to check on Ashlynne. It watched as the young girl survived the horrors both seen and unseen of her world within the confines of the state foster care system.

She sensed that Ashlynne was at a breaking point. Something had to give. Meredith dearly hoped that whatever that was wouldn't be the end of Ashlynne's incredible Light. As much as she wanted to intervene, Mimi had told her in no uncertain terms that she must not. So she and the owl watched and waited to see what the girl would do.

Shrugging into her parka and jamming a knitted cap over her head, Meredith hoisted the tote bag over one shoulder and headed out into the blowing snow to her car. The trip to Tom's would be slow-going with this winter storm, but that suited Meredith just fine. She wasn't looking forward to the meeting at all.

As the Witch piloted her car through the blowing snow of a Northern Michigan blizzard, the young girl she had been watching entered what would be her last foster home, currently hidden from the road in the white-out of the same storm. Ashlynne Barrow was a teenager now and shone as bright as ever. Although, the daily horrors had piled up and weakened her resolve to help the younger children. Her previous attempts at intervention on their behalf had not gone well over the years, leaving her unsure whether she should attempt any help at all anymore. But Ashlynne could see so much more than anyone else, and that knowledge made it impossible to do nothing.

She would need to figure out how to protect the weaker ones or flee to save herself. There didn't seem to be a third option.

Chapter 25

ell me again why you're just now showing us this magical item and its use?" Tom asked again.

Trying hard not to sigh aloud, Meredith repeated the explanation she decided to use. She knew that to be fully truthful would be voicing her distrust of the High Priest and most of her coven mates.

"I wanted to make sure I fully understood the mechanics and how to use it so I wouldn't pass along harmful or dangerous instructions."

"Yes, but why not tell us about it when you returned home and explain that a lesson would happen soon, that you were still learning?" asked Camryn from the back of the group. Meridith noted that she and Stella were sitting side by side again. The two seemed permanently joined at the hip, and their combined energy proved to be more disruptive than group-oriented. Yet another part of Dark Grove that she dearly wished she could change.

"Would any of you have let that go? If I had told you that I had returned from Scotland with a magical stone that had the power to move items and living things from one place to another?"

"I think you don't want us to learn as much as you. Also, I don't think you will show us how to make our own Journey Stone," said Stella, flatly.

Meredith was momentarily stunned by the other woman's obvious disregard for coven etiquette as well as the blatant accusations.

Meredith raised an eyebrow almost to her hairline and chose her words very carefully.

"Stella. I have to say that your thoughts on this come as a great surprise. I have no reason to hoard magic—it's my job to teach and facilitate you and the rest of the group. As far as making your own Journey Stones, I don't believe it's possible. The one we're using today was gifted to me by a talented Old Guard Witch that I met in Edinburgh. She never said if she had actually created the Journey Stone or if they only present themselves to a Witch every so often. It's not about my willingness to show you how to make one. It's that I, myself, was not instructed or told if it's possible."

There was a steely-eyed but silent standoff between the two women before Riley jumped in with an attempt at breaking the stalemate.

"Let's get something to eat before we begin the exercises," she announced with a large, albeit forced, smile at the group. "I'll get stuff out of the refrigerator if you'll grab the paper plates and plastic silverware," she said to her sister as she physically hauled her up from her position on the floor next to Stella.

"What are you doing?" hissed Riley to her sister as she grabbed paper plates from the cupboard.

"I'm not doing anything! I have questions about why Meredith kept this from us, just like Stella and just like Tom! Why are you jumping on me about it?"

Riley found the plastic silverware and a pile of paper napkins and shoved them toward her sister.

"I'm jumping on you because it seems that whenever Stella says 'jump,' you ask 'how high?' Meredith is our High Priestess and has done nothing to deserve what you and your new *best friend* are putting her through!"

Camryn watched as Riley pulled foil-covered dishes and bowls from the refrigerator and balanced them precariously one atop the other before turning back around to continue her hissing whisper.

"We have been a part of this group since the beginning, and I think you owe Meredith a little more loyalty. I don't like how I see things going, Cam."

"Maybe 'the way things are going' is just the way they need to be, Riley! Maybe the coven is moving in a different direction, and Meredith needs to show *us* some loyalty—or step aside."

Riley stood in the doorway between the small galley-style kitchen and the dining room, watching her sister as she strode to the table and deposited her armload of supplies before stalking back to the living room to rejoin the coven.

Riley took her time setting up the small potluck while she gathered her thoughts and contained her frustration; tensions were running high enough without her adding a sister spat to the coven's boiling cauldron.

Stashing the assorted lids and foil coverings back in the kitchen, Riley hollered out for the group to help themselves and heard them troop into the dining room. From the sounds of their voices, the mood had lightened, for now. Riley was grateful, but the feeling of unease had settled in the pit of her stomach.

"Hey, lady!" called Meredith good-naturedly as she joined Riley on the back deck that looked out over the fields beyond. It was cold, and the wind whipped their hair ferociously, but both women stood huddled under the eaves with a plate of food.

"What are you doing out here in the cold?" asked Meredith, her voice raised over the howling December wind.

"I just needed some air," Riley responded and watched as Meredith's usual stoic expression bloomed into a smile at the irony.

"Well, you're certainly getting plenty of that right now! But how about you come back inside, or at least let me bring you a coat."

"Meredith, are you worried?"

"Worried about what, Riley?" she asked, her tone carefully neutral because 'worried' was Meredith's natural state, something she worked very hard to keep hidden from the group. Best to find out exactly what Riley thought she should be worried about before showing her hand.

"The infighting, Stella, how things are with us all right now," Riley responded, her teeth beginning to chatter from the cold.

Meredith smiled and steered her friend back into the house.

"No, not exactly worried. I'll admit that we're all a little stressed right now, but I'm sure it's just growing pains."

Riley, letting herself be ushered back inside, debated on whether or not she should tell Meredith about what her sister had said. Seeing the easy camaraderie of the group as they entered the dining room, something that had become so rare as of late, she decided against it. For now. At some point she would need to tell Meredith, she told herself. In truth, she was scared—scared of Stella and scared of standing against the coven when all the members seemed to like her so much.

"Come on, everybody! Let's finish this up and get to work on the lesson Meredith prepared for us. I don't know about you, but I'm interested to see how a rock can move things from one place to another!" boomed Tom as he stood and gathered up empty plates, discarded plastic forks, and serving bowls.

Taking his lead, the others cleared the rest of the potluck remains, moved the table back to its normal position, and seated themselves around it, drinks at hand.

Meredith, standing at the head of the table, extracted the stone from its carrying bag and wrappings of black velvet and announced, "This, my friends, is a Journey Stone."

The look on each of their faces was hysterical, and Meredith stifled a snicker. She had felt the same feeling of a let-down when Chloe had first shown it to her.

"That's it?" asked Nathan, his face a mask of scowled confusion.

"Yep—this is it. I know it looks like nothing special, but I can assure you that it is nothing short of astounding once you learn how to use it."

Despite the dubious faces that surrounded her, Meredith pressed on. She was unsure of this whole process but for a different reason than her coven. They doubted that the stone was capable of doing all that she said, while she doubted that it was safe for them to have the knowledge.

But the spirit, Mimi, was adamant that she teach them, and Meredith felt compelled to act on faith that she rarely had—in either the living or the dead.

The afternoon wore on. The light gray of the stormy afternoon moved into the darker gray of the evening as Meredith diligently walked the Dark Grove coven through the intricate spellcasting needed to engage the Journey Stone in its duties as a mover-of-matter. By the time the sky turned a dark violet, most of the coven had the basics of the procedure, though Riley and Stella excelled at the practice already.

"I think you've all just about got this down," smiled Meredith, her exhaustion showing on her face and in the slump of her shoulders.

"I have just one more question!" called Stella as Meredith waved a stick of incense around the stone, allowing the smoke to cleanse the item of the extra energies it had absorbed during the day's activities.

"Stella?" replied Meredith, continuing with her smudge.

"We know, *now*, that the Journey Stone can move things from here to there. We all moved that pencil from the table to the kitchen counter and Tom's book from the shelf and into the basket on the front porch."

"Yes?" asked Meredith, feeling annoyed by the criticism that she hadn't taught them the skill right away, brought up yet again in Stella's tone.

"Yes. So..." continued Stella, her eyes flashing with glee at the tit-for-tat between Meredith and herself. "Can we move a *person*?"

The background murmuring of the other coven members came to an abrupt stop. The resulting silence rang out in its completeness. Even the winter winds seemed to have hushed.

Meredith carefully wrapped her stone in its velvet covering and placed it back into the satin pouch. Goosebumps and chills ran up and down her back, and there was a heaviness in the pit of her stomach. Why did Stella's question frighten her so much? Realistically, it was a perfectly reasonable question if one were to follow the lesson through. She, herself, had considered the squirrel. Yet, she had omitted that from her lessons with the group and had never considered moving a *human,* even during her experiments in Scotland.

Stella watched Meredith's reaction to her question with interest. The Faerie had whispered this idea to her earlier in the lesson, and she had waited until just the right time to plant the concept to both Meredith and the group as a whole. The Faerie whispered many things to Stella, their connection strong enough for communication now that Tom kept the box in the living room where they most often met.

"Someone walk over your grave?" laughed Stella as she watched the High Priestess struggle to contain the dismay and confusion that her question had created.

Chapter 26

eredith woke up with a start and looked around in confusion. Where was she? As the fog of the nightmare faded, she recognized her surroundings. She had only recently decided to move into her parents' former suite across the landing from hers. While her rooms were beautifully decorated, they had been designed with a teenager in mind. Meredith, now well past that age, chose to move rather than redecorate. In reality, she had eight other rooms to choose from, but only hers and her parents' provided a full suite with a bedroom, sitting rooms, closets, and spa-like bathrooms. The other bedrooms were beautiful, but she preferred to have a larger space in which to escape.

She had decided to switch rooms just after the Yule celebrations. She called in the cleaning company that maintained the house and had them do a full top-to-bottom cleaning and dusting of her parents' former space. She had boxed and removed the majority of their possessions herself a year after their deaths, so it wasn't a difficult task for the housekeepers to move her clothing and toiletries from one suite to the other. She should have felt more emotional about changing rooms, but she didn't. She had settled so completely into the role of Mistress of Rosehaven that it was natural for her to assume that suite. She had to admit, though, that she was comforted by the fact that Eliza held no ill will regarding the room switch, gladly turning the lights on and opening the doors for her in her new suite, leaving the more childlike rooms dark and closed.

Meredith swung her legs out of bed and walked carefully over the sculpted wool rug resplendent in hues of soft pink, gray-green, and ivory. Its cascading design of roses and leaves was a testimony to her mother's gardens.

Earlier, she had had a nightmare that left her shaky. If she tripped and broke an ankle, she would have to be carted out of her home by the paramedics. The neighbors would have a field day with that.

Making it to her bathroom without breaking any bones, Meredith filled a glass with water from the tap and drank deeply, pushing the fog in her head further away from consciousness.

"Same as the last one, and the one before that, and the one before that one," she whispered as she pulled on a sweatshirt and sweatpants against the cold of the early morning. Holding her socks in one hand—Amanda's constant reminders to not go up and down the wood stairs in socks lest she fall and break her neck now a permanent refrain in her subconscious—she made her way downstairs and into the kitchen. It was colder on the main floor. After starting coffee, she nudged the thermostat up against the chill of deep winter.

Snuggling into the loveseat in the sunroom and waiting for the sky to lighten with the dawn that was still an hour away, Meredith sipped her coffee and ran through the details of the nightmare again.

It was always the same, but no matter how many times she flipped through the images in her mind, the dream remained a disjointed and confusing visual narrative. It began with her running through a cedar grove. She could see herself as if she was floating overhead. Meredith surmised that she was viewing her dream self from the vantage point of the owl. The terror and anger she felt, though, was completely her own, and it flowed through her like an electrical current.

As she acknowledged these potent emotions, the scene scattered like a dandelion blown apart for a wish. The scene was replaced by her mother's crystal vase that stood in the music room, smashed into a million rainbow-hued shards, and she looked at the distraught face of the housekeeper who had knocked it off its pedestal.

Drops of multi-colored prisms would then fill her vision only to be replaced by the girl, Ashlynne, as a young woman. She covered the furnishings of a neat but modest apartment and closed a suitcase.

As her dream self watched, the redhead and her dog climbed into a taxi. Then her vision became clouded and tunneled. In every replaying of the dream, this part paralyzed her with a crushing feeling of claustrophobia and terror. She could only see the main staircase of her home, but she couldn't move or turn her head. All around her echoed the sound of hooves clip-clopping on the hardwood floors of Rosehaven. In dream after dream, Meredith stayed as still as possible so the thing that walked with hooves wouldn't notice her. Fear, born of knowing that she was prey, was immense and overwhelming. The dream always ended with Stella's laughter ringing throughout her home.

Finally, Meredith's fear was replaced with an anger so intense it burned its way into her waking mind, leaving her shaking and spent. But the sounds of hooves often followed her into wakefulness.

Clip, clop. Clip, clop.

"This dream has got to stop," she muttered as she rinsed her coffee cup and left it in the sink. She couldn't stomach any more of the stuff having consumed almost an entire pot while she waited for the sun to come up and lost herself in fruitless worry about the nightmare that seemed to be coming at a more rapid pace as the weeks went on.

"I need to get some answers about this," she continued, addressing herself, the empty room, and whomever or whatever else chose to listen as she went back upstairs to get dressed.

Meredith wasn't sure why being fully dressed helped her feel more in control, but it always did. Putting the last decorative pillow in its place on her bed, she decided to figure this whole nightmare thing out today. She was tired, literally and figuratively, of being at its mercy.

Settling herself on one of the living room sofas, Meredith closed her eyes and counted backward from fifty as she felt herself sink fully into the meditation that allowed her to travel to other realms and gather the information she required. There was a time when this was a daily practice for her, but the continued drama and tensions of the coven had sapped her of energy and confidence in her own visions.

Having sunk well below the level of her everyday world, Meredith stepped out into the darkness of the astral plane and waited for images or beings to appear.

"Welcome, my friend," she smiled in greeting as her owl coasted through the darkness and lit on her shoulder, the silver cord shining.

The owl blinked slowly and settled in, clucking in contentment when Meredith reached up and stroked its massive head.

The mirror appeared shortly after the owl, the frame gilt and ornate, suspended in the darkness. As Meredith watched, its glass grew hazy and then swirled with smoke, the scent of cigarettes heavy and cloying.

"Hello, Dear."

"Hello, Mimi. I'm hoping that you can help me."

"I can try. It's what I'm here for."

Meredith told her about the dream and its recurrence. The sights, the emotions, all of it.

"And it's always the same," she finished.

"It has begun, Meredith."

"What?"

"The situation that we *must* get right this time. It's why I'm here and why I've asked you to show the coven the Journey Stone. I know that was scary. Thank you for doing as you were asked. It will be both your undoing and your salvation, Dear."

"I'm not interested in talking in riddles. If you already know what went wrong before, why can't you just go back and do it the right way? I've been told over and over again that 'All Time Is Now.' I'm going to assume, at this point, that it's your monk who is the speaker. If what he says is true, then this whole thing seems unnecessarily complicated and cryptic!"

"There are rules to this time-thing, Meredith. I don't pretend to understand most of them. However, Bennette has given me specific instructions, and I'm afraid you and I will need to follow them so this situation can be resolved. There's more at stake here than just you, Dear."

Meredith glowered at the older woman who, in turn, looked back at the Witch and serenely lit another cigarette.

"Within a year from this Imbolc ritual, you will need to travel to New Orleans. You will need to purchase a doll for Riley's birthday. It doesn't matter in what order those two things are done," instructed Mimi.

"What? A year from now? I need help now, Mimi! And why would I go to New Orleans, and why am I purchasing a doll and giving it to Riley? Her birthday isn't until the summer."

"Believe me, Dear. By the time the Imbolc ritual is done, you will be more than happy to take a break. As for the doll, Riley won't keep it for long. That is how it should be." Mimi blew her perfect smoke rings as she allowed this information to settle with Meredith.

When she was sure Meredith understood the what—if not exactly the why—of it all, she continued. "Before you leave, you will need to set up a company for Rosehaven so it can receive guests while you are away."

"How long, exactly, will it take me to find a doll in New Orleans?" asked Meredith, her voice heavy with suspicion.

"Oh, only a week or two. But you will be, um—indisposed—for most of the following summer. You will need to acquire a house manager who will maintain the house and be available for your guests."

"You are out of your mind if you think that I'm opening my home to guests like some kind of fly-by-night motel," Meredith protested.

"I know this is distressing, Meredith, but you don't have a choice. They will come to the house no matter what, and it is much better for you and all of us if you design their accommodations and manage their stay. You must trust me on this."

Meredith gaped at the older woman. Trust her? She'd gone from a kindly, if not a bit brash, spirit to a pushy travel agent who is insisting that Meredith make unwanted trips and allow her home to turn into a hotel for groups unknown to her.

"You will know the group that will occupy Rosehaven."

Meredith spun around at the sound of a new voice and came face to face with a man of indeterminable age, dressed in old-fashioned monk's robes.

"You must be Bennette?" she hissed at him.

"Aye, I am. It's nice to meet you, Meredith."

Meredith spun back around to the mirror and Mimi, her expression fluid with confusion, anger, and fear.

"As I said, Dear, it is beginning again."

Chapter 27

While Meredith struggled to process the information—or lack thereof—that Mimi had given her, Riley and Camryn argued over the roles of Stella and Meredith within the coven's hierarchy.

"I can't believe you can't see that Tom is much more aligned with Stella, Riley! Their rituals are smooth and well done and involve all of us rather than 'The Tom and Meredith Show' we were stuck with originally."

Riley glared at her sister then turned her back to her and continued to put away the clean dishes. Their status as roommates was wearing thin, something they both knew but didn't speak of. There were so many things dividing them at this time that adding their living arrangement to the discussion seemed unnecessary.

"It never seemed to bother you before, having Meredith as High Priestess."

"That's because I didn't know anything else, Riley! But the differences in styles are so obvious. Meredith is dry and runs rituals like a college course. There's energy but no personality. I've watched Tom try to add that over the years, but it always winds up being more about them and their differing approaches than the ritual and us—the coven. With Meredith, we're constantly set aside, just observers of her performances."

Riley stared at the kitchen floor. She didn't know how to respond. She wanted to defend Meredith but wasn't sure how because the person that her sister just described bore no resemblance to the High Priestess that she knew.

Taking a deep breath, she could only ask, "And what about Stella, Cam? What makes her, at only a first-degree Witch, so much better as a High Priestess than Meredith, who has all three cords of initiation, extensive training, and truly cares that we are trained well?"

"Stella is fun. Stella doesn't care about the traditional hierarchy but sees each of us as individuals, not as a robe with colored cords. She tells it like it is and isn't in this for the cords—she doesn't *need* them." Camryn's color was high and her chin lifted, daring her sister to counter her claims.

"Cam, you can't be serious! First of all, for someone who doesn't care about initiation cords, she's about to be testing for her second degree. That aside, the cords mean nothing as plain objects, but as *symbols* they are incredibly important. You know this! They represent spiritual milestones and intellectual growth within our group. What you're describing is like hiring a plumber because you need an electrician. You want an untrained person running our rituals who doesn't believe in training, yet you would have that same person be in charge of our training? This is craziness, Cam!

"I knew I couldn't talk to you. Stella tried to warn me, but I was hoping, as sisters, you could set aside your bias. You know, people will do anything, no matter how absurd, to avoid facing their own soul."

"Jung. You're quoting Jung to me? Camryn! Who taught us about Jung? Meredith did! And your quote is incomplete and out of context. Why are you doing this?"

Riley saw a shadow of a doubt flit across her sister's face, and for just a moment thought perhaps she had gotten through to her, but then it was gone. Instead, Camryn smiled condescendingly at her and left the kitchen. Her reply, tossed casually over her shoulder without even once looking back left Riley speechless.

"Be careful, Riley. This coven can't have two High Priestesses, and I suggest that you get on board with where the real energy lies. See you at Tom's. I'm riding with Stella."

Riley's head spun in confusion. The double speak and half-truths of the conversation left her dizzy, but the implication of it all left her afraid. Though she claimed to not need initiations or the cords that represented them, Stella still planned to follow through with her second-degree ritual.

"Why?" moaned Riley as she dropped into the nearest chair, her hand clutching her forehead where a migraine threatened to bloom in all of its nausea-inducing glory thanks to the go-round with her sister.

"Power," she answered herself. "She may not need the cord, but the ritual itself confers power to the recipient. Oh, Camryn—what have you gotten us all into?"

Chapter 28

February holds within itself the promise of that which is yet to come. The seed buried deep within the cold earth only needs the warmth of spring and gentle rains to allow it to burst forth in all of its fecundity. Some say that the seed of what will be is a beautiful daisy or a deep red rose, but not all seeds grow to be sweet. Sometimes that which will be, held deep within the still coldness of February, is the darkly seductive Datura. The flowers hang, heavy with poison, from its green trailing vines and promise wisdom and knowledge but provide only fear and paranoia to those that trust it to tell the truth of a matter. Imbolc holds these energies within the Witches' spring rituals. Side by side with the emergence of hope and light lies the quickening of a cancer. Unlike the beautiful rose, no feeding is necessary for the unease to thrive. Simply doing nothing will provide the necessary space for the malignancy to choke out all that is good and healthy.

What is most important for those living through the perils of February is to remember that despite the unknown plant within the seed, it is certain doom to deny the call of Imbolc which urges us to move, grow, thrive, and be brave. It reminds us that with the coming of the sun, we must stretch ourselves and be strong, no matter the cost.

Ashlynne Barrow had had enough of the horrors she was forced to witness and made her escape. It was cold outside. February in Northern Michigan was a miserable time, but it seemed she could endure the foster care system no longer.

The owl peered through the large living room window of the house while obscured by the branches of a large white pine. The redhead jammed a wool beanie over her hair, wrapped a scarf around her neck, and shrugged into a heavy parka that looked two sizes too big for her. A disreputable backpack containing a few changes of clothes, some granola bars, and what little identification she had was slung over one shoulder as she stuffed her feet into winter boots and headed for the front door. Looking around carefully to make sure no one was about, she slipped out into the predawn morning and made for the trees that surrounded the house. She wouldn't worry so much about being caught if it weren't for the food and paperwork that she had stolen. She felt guilty that she didn't feel bad, but she had put in more labor than she ever received in care. So, lifting a few snacks and the identification that was rightly hers was a necessity, as well as a valid payback for her years of service to the toxic system. The girl who shone so brightly planted her seeds for growth deep within herself as she set off down the two-lane highway headed south and to whatever a life of her own making would hold.

Meredith felt the return of her owl and sat down on the side of her bed to watch the images the bird sent to her. Ashlynne was leaving. Meredith feared for her safety in the cold and windy February ahead, but it wasn't only the girl that she feared for. Ashlynne's leaving meant that whatever situation that she, herself, had been dragged into was progressing.

"A year," she whispered, looking out at the steel grayness of the sky. "A year from this Imbolc. I wish I understood more of this. I feel like I've been strapped onto a runaway roller coaster and blindfolded to boot."

Mentally wishing Ashlynne well on her journey, Meredith headed for the shower.

Like it or not, the ritual this afternoon was still on despite the awful weather and Meredith's equally awful mood. Elevating Stella to a second-degree Witch seemed like nothing less than letting a fox into the henhouse. Despite her objections in multiple meetings with Tom, her reservations and concerns were dismissed, if not outright ridiculed.

Meredith stood under the hot spray of water, letting it loosen her tight shoulders and massage her scalp. Weeks of worry had left her muscles tight and her head perpetually aching.

"You'd better get a hold of yourself because if what Mimi and the monk say is true, you have a year more of this," she said as she lathered shampoo into her hair, listening to her voice bounce back to her from the shower's tiled walls.

Then it hit her, and no amount of hot water could stop the chills of fear that ran up and down her nude body. A year to set the situation to rights. A situation that she did not have any details about but was apparently dire enough to gather the attention of a monk and spirit who could kidnap a Witch for their own uses. She had forgotten to ask the most important question of all, so caught up was she with her indignation of her home being overrun with carpetbaggers.

Will she be alive at the end of this year?

Meredith stepped out of the shower and wrapped her shivering body in a towel. Wiping away the steam from the mirror, she peered at her face, drawn and pale despite having just been in a shower hot enough to fog up the entirety of her suite.

"Step carefully from here on out, Meredith. You didn't crawl through the wreckage of loss to be sacrificed on the altar of someone else's cause."

The Witch, powerful beyond even her own reckoning, planted her seeds of survival. The spirits of Imbolc wrapped them in swaths of spring green and tucked them away from the harsh February winds until the warmth of the coming sun would set them aglow with the light of the magic that they held within.

Chapter 29

Meredith stood to the left of Tom and watched as the rest of the coven filed into the living room-turned-ritual space. They arranged themselves in a semicircle with herself and Tom, flanking the altar, at the head. Unlike other rituals, the altar had not yet been cleansed or consecrated—though its accouterments were in place—and the quarter energies were not called nor the circle cast. The ritual would convey the second-degree cords of initiation to Stella and would require her to perform these duties without the aid of notes or help from the coven. Meredith dearly hoped that she would fail.

With a nod from Tom, Meredith rang the brass handbell in three sharp clangs, signaling the start of the ritual.

From the dining room, Riley led a robed and blindfolded Stella into the living room and to the edge of the circle of her coven mates.

"Who comes to us?" intoned Michael, issuing the first of the ritual challenges.

"Stella," came the reply from the blindfolded woman.

Michael lifted a dagger from the edge of the table closest to him and held the point to Stella's breast.

"Only a proper person, properly prepared, may enter the circle. How do you enter?"

"In perfect love and perfect trust," replied Stella, her words strong and dropping like stones into the stillness of the group.

"Do you enter of your own accord? For it would be better for you to fall on this blade than to enter with fear or reservation within your heart," said Michael, continuing the scripted challenges.

"I come to you with no fear and no reservation. I come in perfect love and perfect trust," said Stella, reciting the response.

Meredith watched closely. At no other time did the call and response seem so fraught with hidden meaning, but Stella stood tall and serene, confident, yet appropriately humble. It was infuriating.

"All those who come in perfect love and perfect trust are doubly welcome," continued Michael.

Riley stepped closer to Stella's back and said, "I give you a third password to pass through the door and into the sacred space—a kiss." She leaned forward, kissed Stella lightly on the cheek, pulled off her blindfold, and pushed her roughly into the circle, signifying the change between the mundane world outside the circle and the magical one within it.

Stella stumbled before catching her balance. The initiating Witch is not warned in advance of this push, as it is meant to be jolting. Meredith had never felt such amusement in watching the act as she did now.

Careful not to let her amusement show on her face, she rang the brass bell three times more, signaling Riley to stand next to Michael and complete the circle, then motioned for Stella to approach the altar.

"You have come to us properly prepared and in perfect love and perfect trust. Your tasks will now begin."

"You must perform all components of the ritual circle in order to wear the second-degree cords and call yourself Priestess within this coven," continued Tom as his role dictated, his voice booming and bouncing around the small room.

"Are you willing to perform these tasks in the presence of your coven, your High Priest and High Priestess, the Mighty Ones, and the Gods?"

"I am," replied Stella.

"Then you shall begin with the consecration and blessing of the altar," said Meredith, carefully modulating her voice to not give any indication of her hope for the other woman's failure.

Stella began, seamlessly moving through the physical and vocal requirements necessary to cleanse, consecrate, blend, and finally activate the energies of the ritual tools.

Tom watched, pleased with her command of this first task. Meredith simply nodded before raking the rest of the coven with her eyes, silently requesting their verdict. She watched as each silently nodded their assent. While frustrated, she couldn't find fault with their decision; Stella's task was performed flawlessly.

"You have been found proficient in the cleansing and consecration of the altar by your coven mates, your High Priest, and your High Priestess. You may continue to the circle call, beginning with the quarters," directed Tom.

Stella stepped away from the altar and closed her eyes. She planted her bare feet firmly onto the carpeted floor and breathed deeply.

Listening to the wail of the wind outside the windows, Stella gathered her energy and grounded her nervousness. She had practiced this for months.

Her voice rang out, louder than probably necessary, as she moved from quadrant to quadrant calling and summoning the energies of the East, the South, the West, and the North that would both guard and anchor the energies of the magic circle in this time and place.

Having concluded that portion of the task, Meredith watched as Stella stepped to the Northern quadrant and took a deep breath.

She felt the amount of theatrics employed was not at all necessary, but she could tell by the expressions on Tom's and the coven's faces that they were all impressed.

Stella began the circle call. She raised her right arm and pointed her index finger out straight, visualizing a stream of glittering blue coming from it and landing just outside of the circle of coven members so they would be contained within it.

Moving clockwise, she intoned, "I conjure thee, oh circle of power, that you will be for me a boundary between the world of men and the realms of the Mighty Ones; a meeting place of perfect love and perfect trust contained herein! I call on the spirits of the East, and of the South, and of the West, and of the North, and all ye in the realm of Faerie to aid me in the consecration of this circle!"

She spiraled ever inward and continued, "In the names of the Old One's I consecrate this circle!"

Stella had now reached the center of the circle.

"...and legions await my words!" she shouted triumphantly and stomped her bare foot three times on the floor, sealing the circle and the energies she had stirred within it.

Meredith's jaw dropped. The sheer audacity of the woman to not only put on this ridiculous show but to add phrases to the coven's canon was beyond incredible!

Tom stared in awe at the robed woman who had so completely commanded the energies, as did the rest of the coven. So amazed were they all that no one noticed as Camryn stepped aside, carrying the ritual blade that Michael had used to challenge Stella's entrance.

No one noticed when she traced a large circle in the air at the western quadrant of the circle, whispering the words that allowed for a doorway into the sealed ritual circle.

Everyone noticed, however, when she returned to the circle and closed the door to seal it once again.

Camryn stepped to the center carrying the antique box of Tom's, brought it to where Stella stood, and presented it to her with a slight bow.

Stella held the box aloft and turned in a slow circle, presenting it to the coven.

"What the hell is going on?" barked Meredith, completely confused by what was happening.

"Stella!" called Tom over the coven's combined questions and babble of surprise and confusion."What are you doing? Why do you have the box?"

"Why do you have the box, and why were words added to the ritual?" clarified Meredith, her alarm turning to a white-hot anger. To misrepresent oneself in ritual was unheard of.

Stella turned to Tom and Meredith and smiled triumphantly,"... 'and all ye in the realm of Faerie.' Why, Meredith, were those words omitted from every circle call that you've done? What did you not want us to know or learn?"

Meredith's jaw dropped, then snapped closed in a failed attempt to conceal her confusion.

"Tom and I discussed it during my training. I felt that it was an unnecessary addition to the ritual. We already summon and call in the quarter energies as well as the Gods. Why add the myths of Faerie to it? Right, Tom?"

Tom stood there, watching Stella and the box that she held. Drab green tendrils of mist seeped from the edges of the seams and drifted down onto the carpet.

"Tom! Tom, tell them. You were OK with the changes!" Meredith heard the pleading tone in her voice but no longer cared. The energy within the circle and from the coven could only be described as rancid, and she wanted dearly to run. But she, too, saw what was coming from the ancient wooden box and was frozen in place—her heart hammering within her chest, her eyes bugging from their sockets in terror.

Stella sat the box on the floor and stepped back as the dull green miasma flowed outward, gaining shape and form.

Riley felt ill as the dense fog that flowed from the box, but both her sister and Stella chuckled in anticipation.

Rose tucked her head under Nathan's arm, which he had draped protectively around her as the thing gained substance and began to laugh, a deeply disturbing sound.

As the Baobhan Sith stretched its arms over its head and wiggled in joy, having acquired its physical body once again, Michael let out a screech of terror at the beautiful woman with the cloven-hoofed feet that now stood before them. Her eyes shone as green as glass, and her fingernails were as long and as sharp as daggers.

"Oh my god, Stella. What have you done?" whispered Tom.

"Everyone wants a mystery solved, but no one wants to look it straight in the face," sneered Stella. "This, Tom, is what was held captive in your father's box. This is what you've asked for."

And with that, the circle broke. Nathan, still cradling Rose, ran from the room, followed quickly by Riley, Michael, and finally Tom. Only Meredith and Camryn remained as the Baobhan Sith stepped up to Stella and bent her head until her left ear nearly touched her left shoulder, smiling all the while in hungry delight.

"Thank you, my dear," chuckled the Faerie in a cruel parody of Mimi as it stared at Meredith. As it raked its nails down the flesh of Stella's neck, bringing up beads of blood,

Camryn went white as a death shroud. When the Faerie dipped its head to lap Stella's blood like a cat to a bowl of cream, Meredith's eyes rolled back in her head and she dropped to the carpet, arms and legs akimbo.

Chapter 30

Meredith walked along the beach below the cliffs of Rosehaven, the cold winds of May helping her remain focused. It had been over six weeks since the Imbolc ritual and she couldn't seem to keep her thoughts going linearly. Instead, they skittered and skipped across her brain, inevitably looping back around to that day. That was when she could stay awake. She had taken to walking over ten miles a day along the rocky shores of Lake Michigan to keep from sleeping the days away.

She bent and picked up a flat disk of a stone and whipped it expertly across the water, counting the number of times it touched down and then bounced back up to continue its flight across the dull gray waters.

"Six. That's not a very good one," she said to the seagull that sat beside her with flat black eyes. She continued her walk.

Meredith Cadwell was in a bad way. The trauma of Stella releasing the Baobhan Sith from its box and the resulting reorganization of the Dark Grove coven had left her stunned and shaken. The partial shunning and, almost, exclusion that the group had doled out since then kept her always wondering if she was still a member. Her place as High Priestess had been kicked to the curb by the unspoken agreement of the group, though her continued attendance seemed less agreed upon. Meredith knew for a fact that there were rituals in place to psychically cut someone from the coven as well as the larger clan, but none of those had taken place. She would have felt them.

"Cowards," she hissed into the wind for at least the thousandth time since her world had fallen apart.

"They lack the strength to oust me, so they're making it uncomfortable enough so I leave on my own. I refuse to make it easy for them. If they want me completely gone, they will have to follow through with the magic and make it so."

The anger was ever-present. This furious soliloquy was nothing new, only serving to spin her in circles. She knew this, of course, but it hadn't stopped the cycle.

She was unsure how to proceed, and that was the problem. She was angry and hurt enough to not want to make the process easy for the coven. Of course, making it difficult for them also made it difficult for her. That was the nature of spite.

If she were to be perfectly honest, it was feeling hurt that made it all so difficult. If she were only angry, she would set the bridge alight and walk away laughing, but these people were her family. If she left, she would have no one.

Meredith climbed the wooden steps that scaled the cliffs as she made her way back to her house, the never-ending thoughts about Dark Grove continuing to take up space in her head.

She knew they weren't inviting her to all the coven meetings, and they knew that she knew. She had used her skill as a seer to watch the group and had seen them gathering to invoke the Faerie and watched in continual horror as it drank the blood of Stella, Dark Grove's new High Priestess. Meredith could not understand why this was done and what the coven hoped to receive from this being. And to see Tom stand mute in the face of Stella's regime made even less sense. As to why they allowed her to overlook their activities, Meredith suspected it was meant to convey with certainty that she was no longer an integral part of the coven. Since Dark Grove had ceased to have an outer court group several years ago, she couldn't even claim that membership. At best, she was a shamed congregant, at worst a scapegoat.

While watching the coven, Meredith had heard the accusations against her and felt terribly hurt. How could she be accused of such insanity? Michael claimed she had entered his dreams and terrorized him until he warded his bedroom, and Rose insisted she had seen Meredith's double smiling eerily into their living room windows from outside of hers and Nathan's house. Of course, Stella knew that none of this was true but gathered the accusations with vigor and laid them as evidence of Meredith's unfitness at Tom's feet.

As the accusations grew and became more and more bizarre, Meredith's hurt curdled into a fury so white hot that she was surprised that it hadn't set her hair on fire.

"I thought spectral evidence was done with the Puritans," she growled.

"I guess, in a way, there is some truth to

the idea of it since I *have* been spying on them," she continued with a chuckle that would have most of the coven running for cover.

"But that's fine. I will continue to attend the few gatherings I'm told about and watch the rest from a distance. There can't be any good ending to what Stella has done, and I want a clear warning before the magical shit really hits the fan. I have a little less of a year more of this, according to the spirit and the monk, and I fully intend on being alive at the conclusion of it all."

Entering her home from the back door, Meredith peeled her coat and hat off and draped them over the railing of the stairs that led to the lowest level of the house.

The sleepiness that came unbidden so often now washed over her with the warmth of the home's heated interior, but she shook it off and walked briskly through the kitchen and dining room and up the main staircase to her rooms. Tom had deigned to invite her to the coven's gathering this evening. Apparently, a new member was being welcomed ahead of his dedication ritual.

"So, Bennette, we will finally meet in *my* here and now," she said as she flipped through hangers in her closet, looking for something comfortable yet stylish. She wasn't about to show up looking like the hell they had put her through.

Settling on a pair of black jeans and a gray slouchy sweater, Meredith applied enough makeup to conceal how haggard her face looked, but not enough to look like she had tried to dress up.

"I would rather be drawn and quartered than they know how much this has taken from me!" she hissed as she pulled black leather boots over her jeans and gathered her belongings for the evening.

As Meredith's car pulled out of the

driveway, Stella hurried up the sidewalk from the opposite direction.

Watching the car as it turned the corner onto the main street, she walked purposefully to the service door and unlocked it with the key that she had taken from Tom's house last week. She moved with confidence and certainty in case a nosy neighbor happened to look outside and notice someone skulking around Meredith's house.

Not taking any time this visit to admire the grandeur of Rosehaven, Stella ran quickly up the back staircase and turned right at the second-floor landing to Meredith's suite. Praying that the door wasn't locked, she turned the glass knob and was rewarded by the heavy door swinging soundlessly inward.

"You really shouldn't trust us all quite so much," laughed Stella as she walked through the bedroom and into the sitting room. Sitting under the large window was the small carved chest that Meredith had so nicely described to the coven as the place where she kept her ritual supplies.

Kneeling before it, Stella lifted the lid and inhaled deeply as the mingled scents of patchouli, lavender, lemongrass, and dragon's blood drifted out from the inside of the trunk.

She carefully moved aside sticks of incense, assorted candles, and baggies of dried herbs until she found the purple satin bag where Meredith kept the Journey Stone.

Stella smiled, "There you are!"

She unwrapped the stone from its swath of black velvet and set it on the floor. From her coat pocket, she took a beach stone that looked exactly like Meredith's magical specimen, wrapped it in the velvet, placed it back into the satin bag, and replaced everything within the trunk exactly as it was.

Pocketing the Journey Stone, Stella retraced her steps out of Rosehaven and back to her car that was parked a block away. If she hurried, she could make it to Horton Bay shortly after Meredith's arrival. She smiled with the knowledge that she was well on her way to becoming the new Mistress of Rosehaven.

Eliza watched as the small woman with dark curls pulled through Meredith's trunk and swapped out the stones. Once again, the ghost tried to send the waves of anger that she felt at the woman in an attempt to make her leave, and once again, she failed. Stella's spiritual shields remained as strong as ever.

Chapter 31

I t had been several months since Bennette was introduced to the coven and his formal dedication ceremony. Meredith had attended his informal introduction but not his dedication. Of course, he knew the reason why, but couldn't let on. When he inquired, as he was expected to do, he was regaled with stories of Meredith's malignant escapades and attacks on the other coven members. At each telling, he watched as the members bonded more completely over the combined hatred of their shared enemy.

"Having an 'other' is one of the most powerful group magics that exists and one employed by every religion and civic group from time immemorial," he grumbled as he got dressed and ready for a study group meeting with the Dark Grove.

Being only a Dedicant, he wasn't invited to the Sabbat or Esbat gatherings, only to the informal study groups. Because of this, he had not yet seen the Baobhan Sith. But the reverberations of its release from the box had been felt throughout many realms. Also tolling through the spiritual planes was the continued disease that infected the group mind of Meredith's former coven. Few knew or understood the power sent out when a spiritual group acted as one entity. Beings of both lightness and darkness responded to the vibrations and hearkened to their call. When the vibrations changed, that was also noticed and attended to by whatever best moved and shimmied in tandem with the group.

"Ever Mind The Rule of Three, What Ye Send Out Comes Back To Thee," whispered Bennette. Truth be told, though he knew the outcome of his presence in this production, he felt bad for the coven members. Meredith gave them valuable information and pragmatic road maps to safely navigate the magical life, and they had chosen instead to follow an impetuous woman whose only concern was for her personal gain. She would use the coven and anything else to get what she desired and had no consideration for those who would be lost along the way.

Tonight's study group would focus on constructing and maintaining thought forms. Bennette cringed at the implications of this; either Stella would successfully create and direct hers or Bennette would fail again in his self-appointed mission to destroy the Fae that had taken everything from him so long ago.

He had had a long time to reflect, several lifetimes in fact, and he didn't enjoy the fact that he had become the hypocrite. While deriding Stella for casting her coven mates at the feet of the Faerie for her own benefit, he had done the same with Vera and was now asking the same of Meredith. He had made Mimi into a co-conspirator, resulting in himself, Mimi, and Meredith all manipulating Ashlynne into the very danger that Mimi had died trying to prevent.

"Circles within circles and plans without end," he murmured as he closed his apartment door and walked to the corner to wait for his ride. Michael, living only a couple of blocks away, had agreed to pick him up so they could ride together to the study group. Bennette didn't drive, nor had he any interest in learning the skill. Because of this, he had hoped to secure lodging in Horton Bay so he could walk to Tom's house, but the only apartments available were in the town of Petoskey. Not ideal, but it was only for a short while. Then, he could return to his own place and time. He wondered if they would welcome him.

Chapter 32

Meredith desperately tried to focus on what Rachael was saying, but her eyes kept twitching back and forth between the dining room behind the pretty older woman and the tables to each side of them. She had seen the wolf now for weeks; sometimes it would be right there in a group of people, though none of them saw it, and other times she would see it skulking around the back gardens of her house. The first time she saw it was after the first nightmare. Jolting awake from the familiar but still terrifying dreamscape, she saw the massive head of a wolf looking around the door frame at her. It was so solid and real that she clambered to the very head of her bed, smashing herself against the headboard, and dialed 911 from her cell phone, positive that a wild animal had somehow gotten into her house.

As the operator answered and asked where her emergency was, the wolf disappeared. It didn't dissipate or become diaphanous. It simply winked out of view.

"I-I'm sorry. I must have dialed by accident," Meredith stammered into the phone, then hit 'end' before the operator could ask any questions that she honestly had no answers to.

"Meredith! Hey, you there?" asked Rachael, waving her hand in front of Meredith's face.

"Oh! Oh, yes. I'm sorry!" said Meredith, her face flushing in embarrassment. Being on the lookout for the wolf had become so much a part of her life now that she tended to lose herself in the act.

"I guess I was just daydreaming a little. I am so sorry, Rachael. Would you mind repeating what you just said?" Meredith smiled warmly at her late mother's best friend—the only person from the time before her parents' deaths that still kept in touch.

"I was wondering if you would consider joining the Historical Society? Your parents were always so active, and I know you could be as much of an asset to us as they were."

Meredith was savvy enough to hear 'your donations could help' in between Rachael's polite invitation, but she didn't mind. Providing a large enough donation that would help to smooth over her non-attendance would suit her just fine right now. She could barely follow a luncheon conversation, let alone commit to showing up at a scheduled history group.

"I would be honored, Rachael. Thank you so much for asking me!" smiled Meredith, adding as much enthusiasm as she dared without sounding as off-kilter as she felt. While Rachael had extended the invitation to

join the town's Historical Society, Meredith
could see the wolf gliding through the sea of
chairs in the dining room of the restaurant—
the other patrons oblivious to the hideous
thing that crept through their midst.

"Oh, I'm so glad you've agreed to come on
board! I'll send the admissions paperwork to
the house. You can fill it out along with the
dues and send it back to the office. You'll be
just in time for the September meeting!"
Rachael clapped her hands together like a
small child who had just received the best
birthday present ever. Meredith envied her
easy happiness and lack of guile. While
decades younger, Meredith felt old, worn out,
and jaded. And terrified.

She knew Stella had been sending the wolf.
Over the summer, Meredith observed Dark
Grove's activities, so she knew they had been
working with the creation of thought forms.
Most of the group had crafted a satisfactory
manifestation of their will, though it surprised

Meredith that Bennette seemed unable to accomplish this task. Stella, however, had been the break-out star of the practice, conjuring her wolf and consistently sending it out to accomplish her requests—bringing it back in when those tasks were accomplished.

"Of course she had," muttered Meredith.

"I'm sorry. What did you say?" asked Rachael, looking at the younger woman over her menu.

"I said, of course, they have it!" smiled Meredith, quickly recovering. "Of course, they have fresh walleye today!"

"Yes, I see that. I think I'll have the chicken salad, though. Walleye is a little heavy for lunch," responded Rachael.

"I guess I'll have the same," said Meredith, trying to sound interested in what she would eat as she waved for the server.

Both women, having placed their lunch orders, chatted about this and that, as one does at a luncheon. Social convention dictates that it's best to not bog down a lady's lunch with heavy or sad topics.

Meredith knew that to mention ghosts wearing top hats and spectral wolves roaming about was also frowned upon in polite society, so she remained quiet about these topics and talked instead about how nice the city's gardens looked this summer and whether the fall leaves would peak before the October winds tore them all from the tree branches.

She absolutely did not mention that the man in the top hat was most assuredly a spirit because he was the only one in the dining room who could see the wolf aside from Meredith. Additionally, she uttered not a peep about how the top-hatted spirit threw a white linen tablecloth over the wolf, effectively sending it back to its Mistress.

"Oh my! That poor boy! Imagine having to carry such a heavy load of linens up and down the stairs all day long!" said Rachael as she watched the crisply laundered and folded tablecloth from the top of the busboy's stack slide off the pile and float to the ground where it briefly held a vaguely animistic shape before settling onto the carpet.

"Yes, imagine that," replied Meredith dryly.

"Well, I'm glad you chose the Weathervane for our lunch! There's never a dull moment here!" laughed Rachael, taking a sip of her wine and smiling at her dearest friend's daughter.

"I'm glad, too," said Meredith, smiling both at Rachael and the man in the top hat. "The Weathervane is always such a lovely place to relax."

Chapter 33

As it turned out, Meredith need not have given much thought to the autumn leaves of Northern Michigan. As the summer wound down and her fear ramped up, she decided it was time to get away for a while. She had worked diligently to fulfill the tasks Mimi had given her, including finding a large doll to gift to Riley for her birthday. Arrayed in Victorian finery with an elaborate feathered hat atop its dark coiffed hair, Meredith thought it was the perfect gift for someone who collected dolls. Meredith had it wrapped and sent to Riley's apartment with a card, wishing her all the best since they rarely saw each other anymore, and Meredith was unsure where she stood with her friend.

When the horrifying suspicion that she might not live through whatever the monk and the spirit had planned bloomed like a poisonous flower in her mind so many months ago, Meredith had made it her goal to put some of the pieces to the puzzle together. She refused to just walk into whatever craziness the monk had set up, blind and unprepared. Throughout the summer, she researched the folklore of the Fae and how contracting with them could benefit—or not—humans. She wrote down the terrifyingly disjointed scenes of her reoccurring nightmare and utilized her owl and her abilities as a seer in an attempt to piece together what had been going on and what they might mean.

She couldn't claim to understand most of it—in truth, even half of it—but it seemed the monk and the spirit planned to set a trap for the creature. While researching the thing that Stella had released from the box, she found that a blood-drinking Faerie was extremely rare. While most scholars assured the reader that these monsters lived only within the hills and glens of the Scottish Highlands, there were obscure texts and bits of correspondence that suggested that at least one Baobhan Sith had escaped its European homeland. Meredith was banking on this being that one.

With her sketchy narrative in mind, Meredith finalized the last of the tasks requested of her and called her attorney to have him set up a property management company for Rosehaven so it could receive guests in her absence. This galled her to no end, but she was beginning to understand a little of what the monk foresaw. She trusted that her home would be better protected as a corporate entity than simply a private residence.

"At least, I hope so," she said aloud as she signed the last of the paperwork to form the property management end of Rosehaven's new corporate status.

Sitting in the puddle of sunshine in her kitchen, she looked around the room that had always been her favorite place in the large house.

"I hope I live long enough to reclaim it as my own home. Gods, I am so damn tired," she sighed as she walked to the service entrance door and slipped the envelope partly outside the mail slot so the mailman would take it.

Climbing the main staircase to her rooms, she retrieved her suitcase from the closet and laid it open on her bed.

"You don't get to decide everything, Bennette. I'm doing as you asked—or demanded—but my trip to New Orleans will be done on my schedule, not yours. I'm sick to my core of that damned wolf and the cryptic instructions from you and your underling, Mimi," she said loudly and with enough of a sharp edge that if either were listening, they would know enough to tread carefully if they chose to engage with her at all.

"I'm terrified of a blood-drinking Faerie. I mean really, Bennette! When had you planned on letting me know about *that* tiny detail?" she continued ranting as she grabbed slacks, blouses, jeans, and t-shirts and stuffed them all into her bag chaotically.

"And while we're at it, do you have any idea what that damn doll cost me? Given the circumstances of what happened between the coven and me, a birthday card to Riley would have more than sufficed and cost a fraction of the doll!" Meredith added socks, underwear, and sneakers to her suitcase before stomping off to her bathroom for toiletries.

"Aye, I know it was pricey, and I thank ye for doing it," came the monk's rolling Scottish brogue.

"Bennette!" screeched Meredith, her heart jumping painfully in her chest as she spun around to see the monk framed in her bathroom mirror. "What the hell?"

"I'm sorry to have frightened you, Meredith. I know you're tired and angry, and I know this has all been a horrific few years for you. I promise I will do everything in my power to bring it to an end as soon as possible."

Meredith eyed him warily, trying to decide if she should give voice to her biggest fear. Deciding to go for broke, she asked quietly, "Does that include my being alive at the end of it?"

Bennette regarded her for several seconds before saying just as quietly, "It is my intent that you come out of it alive, Meredith."

After adding her lotions and soaps to her bag, Meredith zipped it closed and fought back tears of fear and frustration. Bennette only expressed his intention-his hope. In truth, it seemed that he had no idea if that would be the case.

As she bumped her bag down the side service stairs, she wondered if, before she had asked, it had even occurred to him.

As Meredith boarded the small plane that would leave Traverse City's Airport bound for New Orleans, she settled back into her seat and whispered, "I think it's time for me to see my bright girl for myself."

As the Witch's plane took off, Bennette stepped through the full-length mirror in the guest room at the far end of the third-floor hallway, tucked under the massive roof of Rosehaven.

He stood still and listened, the footfalls of the spirit, Eliza, picked up pace as she made her rounds through the large estate.

"Hello, my dear," smiled the monk gently to the ghost that stood silently, watching him from the other end of the long hall.

Bennette sent out his feelings of warmth and friendship to the wandering ghost, letting her know that he could see her and that he meant her no harm.

Eliza's face showed just the smallest hint of a smile, but she didn't flee. So, Bennette continued.

"When next you see me, Eliza, I will need a favor from you. It will be hard to understand, but it will serve the greater good that I am here to fulfill. Are you willing to help me?"

Eliza nodded slowly, not ready to commit entirely to the strange man that had invaded her space.

Bennette smiled and closed his eyes. Forming a series of images in his mind, he sent them out to Eliza. Her eyes opened wide in both surprise at his skill and fear at what she had seen.

The young woman in blue sent back her own thoughts, and Bennette nodded in response.

"I will do everything in my power to protect her—and your home. You have my word," he responded.

Eliza nodded once and vanished, not bothering with the pretense of walking away or constructing the sounds of footfalls. Those were for the Mistress of Rosehaven, and it seemed like that position might be in question now.

Chapter 34

Meredith woke up when the plane bumped down onto the tarmac. Her flight to New Orleans had been uneventful, a blessing after the non-stop eventfulness in her world up to now.

Exiting the plane ahead of the mass of people in line behind her, one of her favorite perks of a first-class seat, she pulled her rolling bag behind her into the brightly lit airport.

The sounds and smells of New Orleans engulfed her as she made her way to the front where her car would be waiting; the jazz piped in on the speakers, a happy counterpoint to the aromas of cayenne and garlic.

Meredith had never been to New Orleans. In fact, besides her trip to Scotland several years ago, she had not traveled at all since her parents' death. Despite having the financial means to go anywhere that she chose, her life revolved around the Dark Grove coven. It was never specifically stated that members curtail their outside interests and relationships, but the secrecy of the coven's workings—as well as the numerous required meetings—made it nearly impossible to have any lasting friendships or interactions outside of the group.

Being on the outside looking in, she was beginning to see how dysfunctional this setup was and how it had helped to create the discord within her coven. That and the fact that, based on her first scrying, the coven should not have been formed at that time anyway. The whole thing was rushed from the get-go, and they were all now sowing what they had reaped—herself included.

"Ms. Cadwell, please follow me," said her driver warmly as she approached the man holding a sign with her name on it.

"Thank you." She returned the smile and followed him outside to the waiting black SUV at the curb.

As the large car rolled down the highway from the suburbs that housed the airport into downtown, Meredith watched the unfamiliar scenery flow past her tinted window. The driver didn't chitchat aside from confirming her hotel, and she was grateful for the silence.

As the massive rounded roof of the Superdome appeared ahead of them, Meredith felt nervous. Who did she think she was, traveling thousands of miles to spy on a young woman who she had never met? Even the justification of having been instructed to come to the city by Mimi seemed hollow and silly now.

"Desperate times and all," she whispered.

The driver expertly piloted the large vehicle off the freeway, and it was followed by an immediate change of scenery and energy. The heightened activity of the airport and the freeway gave way to a languid warmth. No need to hurry, no need to rush, it whispered seductively. Meredith was enchanted.

The warren of streets that made up the French Quarter were no less enchanting, if not a bit more hurried. Visitors in Bourbon Street t-shirts jockeyed for space on the cracked slate sidewalks with black and white-clothed servers hurrying to get to their next shift. Music was everywhere, and it seemed every balcony dripped with greenery.

"Ma'am..."

Meredith smiled as the heavy warmth of the subtropical city wrapped her in its sultry embrace. The doorman ushered her from her car and into the lobby of the Hotel

Monteleone, her bag already whisked away to her suite.

When she knew her dates to leave Charlevoix for New Orleans, she contacted Rachael and asked her to recommend a travel agent to secure rooms for at least a month, maybe longer. She was glad to have trusted the agent with the details.

"Wow, talk about a job well done!" she said as she was shown her suit. The travel agent also had a bit of a sense of humor it would seem, having booked her in the Ernest Hemingway Suite—a sure nod to her Northern Michigan home—though the obvious parallel to Horton Bay and the coven made her a little squeamish. Reminding herself that the travel agent would not know Meredith's direct connection to Horton Bay, she allowed the feeling of unease to float away to be replaced with a happy appreciation of her home for the next several weeks. The Ernest Hemingway suite was a rooftop suite with double balconies and direct access to the pool.

"Ma'am, the adjoining room has been booked in your name as requested. Shall I open the doors for you or leave them locked? Your key card will operate that door as well as the main."

"You can open it. Thank you," said Meredith, grateful that the agent had booked the entire space. She was used to having her privacy and wouldn't want to be kept up or woken early with people just a wall away.

Handing her the welcome envelope with two key cards, room service menus, and concierge information, the soft-spoken bellman nodded his thanks at her tip and let himself out.

Meredith kicked off her shoes and wandered the spacious suite. It was arrayed in a soothing Wedgwood shade of green with toile accents—tasteful and serene. Her bed, a sumptuous king-sized affair, looked so inviting that she had to talk herself out of stripping out of her clothing and climbing between the sheets to sleep away the rest of the afternoon.

The living room featured a forest green velvet sofa, fireplace, and delicate Louis XIV chairs adorned in the green toile that covered the duvet of her bed. The floor-to-ceiling windows that led out to the balcony were hung with heavy custom fabrics that puddled perfectly onto the needlepoint rug that covered the dark wood planks of the floor. An antique chandelier dripping in crystals completed the look.

"Stunning!" smiled Meredith as she opened the windows to the balcony and looked out over the gabled rooftops of the famed French Quarter. "Simply amazing," she sighed.

As Meredith settled into what would be her home away from home for the coming weeks, Stella honed her skills with her thought form—the wolf that had stalked and terrorized Meredith—and the stolen Journey Stone.

More often, she gathered the coven together to manifest the Baobhan Sith, each one hearing what he or she most needed. Their most secret and cherished desires whispered into their ear, though it was from Stella, alone, that it took its nourishment of blood.

If any of them, alone in the dark on a moonless and sleepless night, wondered why they no longer gathered to celebrate the passing of the seasons or to worship their Gods, the bright sun of the next day left them feeling exposed and vulnerable—too afraid to speak out. So, each stayed quiet, finding safety within the group. After all, look at what had happened to Meredith. If the High Priestess could be set aside and hated, then what of each of them? Besides, the Faerie promised more than Meredith could have, or would have dared, and none wanted to lose their portion of the spoils.

As the minute details coalesced around Bennette's needed resolution, he and Mimi monitored the activities of Meredith's former coven and directed her owl on errands, both in this time and in others, to ensure that all details be finalized that would destroy the Baobhan Sith. He couldn't fail again.

Chapter 35

Like so many before her and on down through the centuries, New Orleans completely enchanted and captured Meredith's heart. From the amazing luxury of her hotel to the cracked and broken facades of the old Spanish architecture, she thought she could stay here forever and still not see all there was to see in the thirteen square blocks that made up the neighborhood called the Vieux Carre'.

Her first two weeks passed by in a pleasant, touristy sort of way. She had lunch at Muriel's, then wandered the Louisiana State Museum in the Cabildo as an unexpected rainstorm whipped the banana trees and palms in a frenzied thrashing in the gardens of Jackson Square. Hiring a driver, she spent a long day exploring the sites of the enormous plantations that lined River Road along the Mississippi, offering her silent condolences to the spirits of the grand homes for their terrible mistreatment in the pursuit of riches and status. She even took a late evening haunted history walking tour that proved to be much more fun than she would have ever imagined, partly due to her ability to see the ghosts that the guides regaled about with stories—plus a few others that walked along, enjoying the energy snack of all the tourists.

During several afternoons, she wandered the shops and galleries of Rue Royal, browsing antiques and mass-produced trinkets and drooling over incredible estate jewelry that she would never have an event to wear to, though it was fun to dream. While there was a veritable cacophony of eateries and dining rooms all vying for her attention and patronage, simple coffee and pastries at Croissant D'Or on Ursulines with its old-fashioned tiled interior had become a late-morning favorite.

Meredith meandered through the month of October in a dream of comfort and security. While she missed Rosehaven, she had not felt as well rested and safe in a long time as she did here. The combination of the hotel's attention to service and her distance from the coven helped to lull her into a state of deep contentment.

All of that changed, however, as she lounged by the pool enjoying the sunshine and cool breezes of a November afternoon. Opting for a cheese and fruit plate and a mimosa rather than eating out, Meredith alternately drowsed in the warm rays of the sun and nibbled at her brunch. She had the entire pool area to herself and welcomed the relative silence not found in any other outdoor space within the hyper-occupied downtown.

Replacing the metal cloche that came with her plate of food, Meredith pushed it away and stretched out on the lounger. She was comfortably sated and pleasantly floaty with the effects of the champagne, and she closed her eyes against the bright sun, feeling her body relax.

The sounds that filtered up from the sidewalk three stories below her occupied her brain for a bit and then, slowly, each began to fade until the voices and strains of music from the street musicians became indistinct and no longer a part of her current reality.

Meredith had traveled to the realm from which her owl had provided her so much information over the years, without really trying.

"It must be the weeks of feeling relaxed and well-rested," she whispered into the dark void that spread out around, above, and under her. Her voice sounded hollow and tinny in the vastness.

Meredith, having been to this place countless times in the past, wasn't scared or nervous but intrigued that she had somehow spontaneously traveled.

"Where are you, my friend?" she called into the darkness.

She simultaneously felt the pressure in her chest from her physical body while seeing the owl's winged approach with her astral eyes, a phenomenon that always made her smile at the strange duality of it.

The massive raptor lit on her shoulder; its weight, even in this place, was substantial and heavy.

"Have you called me here?"

The bird blinked its slow blink, then turned its head almost ninety degrees to indicate the intricately framed mirror that hung suspended in the blackness.

Meredith, still holding the owl, walked to the looking glass and stood before it. Within seconds, the glass clouded with lavender mist that floated away, almost immediately showing a group of young adults gathered in a circle under the massive limbs of a southern live oak. The magic circle they had cast glimmered with a shimmering blue that shot up like sparklers from the oyster shells used to denote the space. Meredith recognized Ashlynne but none of the others.

The owl stretched itself on its Mistress's shoulder, spreading its wings wide, and the lavender mist again obscured the vision within the mirror.

"What am I looking at, my friend?" she asked the bird softly.

The owl clucked and clicked in response, and Meredith turned back to the glass to see that the mists had dissipated once again but showed a different scene now. Within the glass, Meredith watched as Ashlynne sat at a table in Jackson Square, a spread of tarot cards displayed in front of her. A woman with dark hair took the seat across from her and smiled brightly. As Meredith watched, the face of the woman blinked in and out like a bad reception on an old-fashioned television set—her human face dancing back and forth with her real visage. It was terrifying. The thing, probably some idea of female, had sickly gray-green skin and hair that looked like the Spanish moss that hung from the great oaks of the southern states. Here and there, within the tangled mass, crawled beetles, roaches, and centipedes, but it was the tiny horns protruding from the top of the thing's head that shook Meredith. By the look on Ashlynne's face, she could also see what the thing sitting across from her truly looked like. Meredith was impressed; to see the being encased within the human body took great skill.

"Morag," the name came to Meredith, unbidden, and with it the full explanation of what it was.

"So my shining girl has Faerie experience, has she?" asked Meredith, no longer sure who or what would answer her. As it turned out, there was no reply at all.

The last image that Meredith saw in the murky glass of the mirror showed the brutal end to which this Fae had come, the hounds that it had once commanded ripping it limb from limb as two powerful entities—one of the Fae and one of New Orleans—watched with a grim detachment.

"You did this. Didn't you, Ashlynne? No wonder I've seen you for so long. Bennette and his spirit, Mimi, have seen far, haven't they?" Meredith's voice was heavy with resentment and admiration at the convoluted plan that must have taken years to sort out.

"Aye, centuries, in fact," came the soft voice from behind her.

Meredith turned and regarded Bennette with an eye to this new information.

"Bennette. Centuries, you say? Where have you come from? Where is your spirit, Mimi, from?"

"The more accurate question would be 'When are we from,' Meredith. Also, Mimi is not my spirit, helper, or underling. You upset her when you refer to her as such."

Meredith caught herself rolling her eyes and forcibly rearranged her face into something resembling contrition, though she didn't feel it at all. What she felt was used and taken advantage of.

"I suppose it's time for me to return to my house, isn't it?"

"Soon. Your escape here to New Orleans can continue for a few weeks more, but after Yule, you will need to be in Rosehaven."

"What happens then?" whispered Meredith sadly. She had almost convinced herself that her time here could last forever.

"Your property management company will need to be instructed to place an advertisement for a House Manager for the upcoming summer—"

"Where am I going this summer?" interrupted Meredith.

Bennette eyed her in annoyance, then continued. "You will be at home, but you will be unable to participate in the events that will happen there. Your House Manager will come equipped with some very unique abilities that will bring all of this to an end by autumn."

Meredith watched him, her mind spinning.

"I have questions, Bennette."

Bennette stood mute, neither encouraging nor discouraging.

"Is it Ashlynne that is coming to my home as a 'House Manager?'" began Meredith, not at all surprised when Bennette declined to react or answer. "Fine. Next then. Will the Baobhan Sith be sent to Rosehaven?"

Again, silence and no reaction from the monk.

Meredith sighed and plunged on, "Will I be alive when this is done in the fall?"

Bennette eyed her carefully, then said, "You have asked this of me before. I do not intend for you to die in this, Meredith."

The Witch stood tall and looked down upon the monk, her ire palpable now.

"Fine, Bennette. Then one more question. Why is Stella so familiar to me? We have not attended any of the same schools, and I can't remember growing up with her in town. I *know* that I know her, but from where? It seems vitally important that I remember!" she finished, almost pleading.

Bennette regarded Meredith, her strong start ending with a desperate plea for information, and felt a pull of pity for her. One more innocent stranded in between an Unseelie Fae and its destructive run through this realm.

He pointed over her shoulder, and Meredith turned back to the mirror. Within the depths of the murky glass, Meredith watched as women, robed and chanting, left a bricked enclosure—each holding a lantern.

"My vision!" she whispered, her blood pounding in her ears.

She already knew what she would see, yet she was powerless to turn away as Stella turned to her astral self that had watched from the side of the original vision and winked viciously.

"Oh, my god. Bennette! Who is she? How did I see her? Why didn't I remember her?" Meredith's question came rapidly, hitting the monk squarely in the chest with their power.

"I don't know all of that, Meredith, but again, your questions might be better answered if you were to ask 'When was she? When was I?' Rather than 'who' either of you were or are."

Meredith came to with a jolt that left her with a sharp crick in her neck and a bad sunburn on her face. She had no idea how long she had been gone, but she needed to get back to her room and write this craziness down. Because when a Witch deems a situation crazy, it is truly bizarre.

The Circle Call: A Witch's Faerie Tale

Chapter 36

Meredith spent the days after she met with Bennette writing the events down in her journal and trying to construct a timeline of all the characters in her personal drama, but it was useless. She simply couldn't wrap her head around the who's, when's, why's, and what for's of it all. She strongly suspected that Ashlynne's encounter with the Faerie, Morag, had already happened, but she had no confirmation of that. So, it remained just another big question mark in her notes.

Finally finding out who Stella was, however, spurred her on like nothing else. The woman may have taken over a group from her before, but Meredith was going to do her best to make sure she didn't do it again.

"I may be able to gather them back into a sane and safe environment," she said to her reflection as she smoothed lotion over the fading sunburn. "Especially if Ashlynne can successfully remove the Baobhan Sith from our world." A scenario that she only inferred from Bennette rather than confirmed.

"I wish I had thought to ask Bennette what Mimi has to do with all this, though he probably wouldn't have said anything anyway," she continued, privately musing as she slipped her feet into a pair of comfortable sandals and stuck her ID and a credit card in her shorts' front pocket.

Her time in New Orleans concluded tomorrow morning, and while she would dearly love to find Ashlynne and catch a glimpse of the girl in real life, she had a strong suspicion that their physical meeting might mess everything up. Meredith dearly wanted to regain her friends in Dark Grove, so she tamped down her curiosity and chose, instead, to explore further uptown by way of the Saint Charles Line Street car. The sun was out, and it was pleasantly warm. She refused to spend her last day in this amazing place plotting characters and timelines in her journal. Even if she wanted to, she realized that she had little control of the reckoning that Bennette was banking on.

The plane lifted off smoothly as Meredith sat back and recalled the best of her time in New Orleans. Though she tried, she couldn't come up with any one individual thing. It was a gumbo of experiences, sights, smells, and places that would have a hold on her soul for years to come. Of this, she was sure.

As with her trip south, she awoke when her plane bumped down on the tarmac, but she now looked at a cold and gray landscape outside her window rather than lush tropical greenery and blue skies.

"I'm back," she sighed as she grabbed her bag from overhead and pulled it desolately out of the plane and into the tiny airport. There was no jazz music and no smell of spices, and Meredith felt indescribably sad.

As her driver pulled up to Rosehaven and she saw the lights on, welcoming her home in the early twilight, her mood picked up a little. While it's true that the cleaning crew that was there this afternoon could have switched on the lamps in anticipation of her return, she knew in her heart of hearts that it was Eliza.

Meredith unlocked the side service door and called 'Hello' to her house, leaving her suitcase at the foot of the stairs. She would bring it up later.

The time change from Louisiana to Michigan had her out of sorts. Though she felt like she should be tired, she was anything but.

"Well, I guess now is as good a time as any," she said to herself and pulled her laptop out of her bag and went into the kitchen. She poured herself a glass of ice water and sat down to send her request to her newly formed property management company, detailing her need for a House Manager for the upcoming spring and summer. Rereading it carefully, she hit send and snapped the laptop closed. In years past, she would be putting away the Yule decorations, but none were put out this year due to her absence. Having run out of things to do, Meredith Cadwell climbed the stairs to her suite and slept in her own bed for the first time in months.

As the days wore on, the grayness threatened to overtake her, so pervasive was it after the warmth and vibrancy of New Orleans. Meredith felt bored and despondent, stuck between wanting to do something and being afraid that whatever plans she made might mess up Bennette's. Out of sheer desperation, she attended a few Historical Society meetings but found herself distracted by her recent questions of time and place. So, she was not a very dedicated participant.

On the last day of December, while the rest of the world got ready for New Year's Eve parties, Meredith sat cross-legged on the sofa in the living room, flipping through the TV channels and trying to find something that would catch and hold her attention.

"I need a hobby," she grumbled as she clicked through home renovation shows, pseudo documentaries about haunted castles, and cooking show competitions.

The sound of the brass mail slot clanking closed got her to her feet.

"Mail!" she laughed, ruefully amused at how easily she was distracted.

Grabbing the pile of assorted envelopes and catalogs from the floor where they had drifted from their fall through the small slot next to the service door, she tucked it all under one arm and went to the kitchen.

Grabbing a handful of almonds, she sat down and sorted through what had arrived. There were copies of bills that the accountants had already paid, seed and flower catalogs, some late-arriving holiday cards from people her parents had known, and a plain envelope with no stamp simply addressed to 'Meredith' in a feminine-looking script.

Meredith popped the last almond into her mouth and slit the top of the envelope with a butter knife.

Inside was a small note card with an image of a candle set into snow, the colors vibrantly blue and green against the pristine white.

She opened the note card, read what was inside, closed it, opened it again, then set it on the table.

The invitation was polite and warm-hearted and should have made her happy. Instead, it chilled her to the bone.

Dear Meredith,

We hope you can attend the coven's Imbolc ceremony on Saturday, February 3rd. Dress warm! We'll be doing a healing ritual at the springs behind Tom's house.

See you soon,

Stella

Meredith read and re-read the note at least a dozen times, and no matter the intended tone, couldn't escape the feeling of imminent danger.

"I have to go, though," she said to Eliza, who she could feel was close by.

"If there's a chance of getting back into the group, I have to attend this. There's no other way."

Eliza's footfalls began on the third floor and moved quickly down to the lowest level, then back up the stairs, only to repeat the route again for the next several hours. Nothing Meredith could do or say could quiet the spirit who watched over the Mistress of Rosehaven.

Chapter 37

The day dawned a lighter gray than the night, the sun so weak that if Meredith hadn't been awake for its anemic advance into the gunmetal sky, she wouldn't have known the difference.

Today was the Imbolc ritual. There were hours yet before she needed to leave, but she was already on her second pot of coffee, having found sleep nearly impossible.

Her stomach swayed with nausea born of both nerves and too much caffeine. "Toast," she mumbled, making her way into the kitchen and pulling the toaster from the cabinet that had housed it for as long as she had been alive.

Spreading the toasted wheat bread with butter and jam, she stood over the sink and nibbled at it cautiously, unsure whether her stomach would accept this meager offering or not.

Gladdened that the toast had, indeed, settled her roiling insides, she dumped the last of the coffee, cleaned up her breakfast crumbs, and made for her bedroom, vacated hours before when sleep had alluded her.

"May as well make the bed and get into the shower," she said as she climbed the main staircase. "It will kill some time, anyway."

Having managed to put away a couple of hours cleaning her bedroom, sorting through her closet for clothes to donate, and changing her sheets, Meredith exited the shower and pulled on jeans and a sweater. If they were going to be outside, there was no reason to be dressed up; the February chill demanded comfort, not style.

Camryn crept quietly into Riley's room. Her sister was a hard sleeper, but she couldn't chance that she would wake up because she had no explanation for why she was taking the doll that had been given to her for her birthday. Stella had instructed her to take it without Riley knowing and Camryn learned that it was often better to do as asked, rather than incur either Stella's or the Faerie's wrath.

Cradling the large Victorian doll, Camryn slipped back down the stairs to where Stella waited. Without a word, she handed it over.

"And to think, it was Tom that I used to be afraid of," whispered Cam as she watched Stella's car back out of their driveway.

From the topmost branches of a dense pine tree, the owl watched all of this and more, able to move in and out of times and places as it pleased. The enormous bird watched Meredith as she paced her house, waiting to leave and save her coven. It watched as

Camryn stole the doll from her sister and handed it over to Stella, and it watched as Stella parked her car a full mile down the road from the off-road to Tom's driveway and trek over the frozen corn fields. She clutched the doll as she made for the copse of cedars and the healing springs.

As the owl saw Meredith's car turn into Tom's long driveway, it blinked its long, slow blink. It watched Meredith exit her car and walk behind the house and toward the springs. It took flight, coasting into the violet mists at the horizon.

Bennette looked out from the full-length mirror that stood in the sitting room of Meredith's childhood suite. The spirit, Eliza, watched his reflection, her expression indescribably sad.

"It is time, Eliza. You know this is the only way," said Bennette to the ghost of the young woman.

Eliza nodded, not in agreement, for she didn't trust Bennette to get her Mistress out of this alive, but in acknowledgment of what she had agreed to. She didn't know if there was another way or not, but if there were, it had not been presented. She would follow the monk's lead.

The crash of the crystal vase as it fell from its pedestal and the cry of dismay by the housekeeper reverberated throughout the estate of Rosehaven but the sobs of the distraught Eliza echoed throughout the realms.

As the sun edged toward the horizon, the sunset showed itself in cotton candy-colored pinks and purple—a rare treat for this time of year. Meredith made her way down the path toward the healing spring, where the Imbolc ritual was scheduled to take place. But instead of her coven mates gathering around the spring and preparing for the event, she found the clearing empty. Turning back toward the path from which she came, thinking that she had arrived early, Meredith saw it—Stella's wolf.

"Stella!" yelled Meredith as she backed up, catching her toes on rocks and roots that erupted from the loamy soil surrounding the springs.

Understanding now that she had been tricked, Meredith stood watching the wolf slink slowly down the path toward her, its tongue lolling from between its razor-sharp teeth.

Meredith planted her feet firmly and called her owl, which erupted from her breast with a ferociousness she had never experienced before. It slammed into the wolf, disrupting its advance.

But Meredith, underestimating Stella and the nature of her attack, had chosen her defense poorly. By sending out everything she had with her owl, she left her physical body vulnerable.

"Meredith," whispered the other woman.

Stepping into the clearing, Stella raised her hands over her head, fingers splayed as dark red and black energy sparked between her palms.

Stella chanted, and Meredith's blood ran cold.

"No! Stella, please. Don't do this!" cried Meredith, hating the weakness in her voice but unable to hide her terror at what was happening.

Stella maintained her position of power, despite Meredith's pleas, and reached into her coat pocket for the banded egg-shaped stone that would rid her of her predecessor once and for all.

Meredith backed up, trying to stay out of reach of the Journey Stone's magic, but stopped short when she saw the doll propped up against the trunk of an ancient cedar tree just off the trail.

"Stella, wait! Why—"

Stella strode quickly toward Meredith before she could finish her question, grabbed the doll, and dropped it in the path between them. She finished the incantation to complete the spell with a triumphant scream, and Meredith felt the full brunt of the other Witch's anger, jealousy, and desire. Before the nothingness consumed her, Meredith sent an arc of magic born of her sadness and betrayal in an explosion of blue light up the trail and directly into Tom's house. There, the Dark Grove coven gathered for an informal potluck, unaware of Stella's and Meredith's meeting at the spring.

Stella called her wolf back and spat on the doll at her feet.

"You can never just let things go, can you, Meredith? Always with the last word. It never fails!" she screamed as she kicked the doll into the brush on her way back up the path and toward the burning structure that lit up the February sky.

Meredith landed with a thump, trapped inside the doll that she had purchased as a gift for a friend that was anything but.

As her prison settled in around her, Meredith, having no idea how to escape, retreated into her own thoughts. She allowed the darkness of oblivion to flow over her like water.

Bennette, surrounded by the rest of the Dark Grove Coven, watched as Tom's house burned to the ground. As the structure caved in on itself—an apt representation of the group as ever there was one—he turned and walked up the long driveway toward the village of Horton Bay. He had much to do before Ashlynne's arrival at Rosehaven.

The End

April 26, 2023

Treme, New Orleans LA

<<<<>>>>

Annie Russell